Her Evil Twin

POISON APPLE BOOKS

The Dead End by Mimi McCoy

This Totally Bites! by Ruth Ames

Miss Fortune by Brandi Dougherty

Now You See Me . . . by Jane B. Mason &
Sarah Hines Stephens

Midnight Howl by Clare Hutton

Her Evil Twin

by Mimi McCoy

POISON APPLE

SCHOLASTIC INC.

New York   Toronto   London   Auckland
Sydney   Mexico City   New Delhi   Hong Kong

ISBN 978-0-545-33325-2

12 11 10 9 8 7 6   12 13 14 15 16/0

Printed in the U.S.A.   40
This edition first printing, April 2011

Her Evil Twin

Chapter One

The note landed on Anna Dipalo's desk halfway through English class. It was written on regular lined notebook paper and folded into a tidy, tight little triangle. Penciled across the front in neat box letters were the words FOR ANNA (PRIVATE!).

Anna glanced up at the front of the classroom. Her English teacher was busy diagramming a ridiculous sentence about someone named Percival and his pet parakeet, so Anna slid the note into her lap and unfolded it. It read:

> You have been chosen.
> Meet in the old girls' bathroom behind the gym.
> 3:10 p.m. Don't be late.

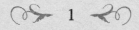

The note was unsigned. Anna glanced around the classroom. Other kids were sneaking glances at their cell phones, doodling in their notebooks, or staring vacantly into space. There was no clue where it had come from.

Anna carefully refolded the note and was about to slip it into the pocket of her jeans when she saw that Jessamyn Ito was twisted around in her seat, looking right at her. When their eyes met, Jessamyn gave a tiny nod. Then she turned back around and faced the chalkboard as if nothing had happened.

Anna felt a rush of excitement that went all the way down to the tips of her toes. Jessamyn was one of the coolest girls in the seventh grade at Woodrow Wilson Junior High. And now she'd chosen Anna. For what, Anna didn't know yet. But she couldn't wait to find out.

At lunchtime, Anna showed the note to her best friend, Dory Welch. She reasoned that the note hadn't *specifically* said not to show it to anyone. And besides, she told Dory everything.

Dory read it through twice while she ate a cheese sandwich. When she was done, she set down the sandwich and pushed her glasses up on her nose. Dory wore big, round glasses with thick lenses. They made her hazel eyes look huge.

"I don't know," Dory said.

This was not the response Anna had been expecting. "What do you mean, you don't know?"

"I mean, I don't know if you should go. It might be a trick," Dory replied.

Anna frowned. "A trick?"

"Remember at the beginning of the year when Jessamyn and her friends gave Claudia Wheaton a free cherry slushie — with ketchup and mustard mixed in?"

How could Anna forget? Claudia had drunk three giant gulps before she'd realized, and then she'd gotten violently sick all over the cafeteria floor. Everyone had talked about it for days afterward.

"Okay, that was kind of mean," Anna admitted. "But Claudia shouldn't eat every single thing that gets put in front of her." She didn't say what she was really thinking, which was, *But Claudia is a dork. And I'm not.*

"It says here you're chosen," Dory said, pointing to the line in the note, "but it doesn't say what for. Don't you think that's a little weird?"

"Well, obviously they want me to join a club or something," Anna said impatiently. She was starting to regret showing it to Dory.

"Why would Jessamyn choose you to join a club?" Dory asked. "It's not like you're friends."

The question irked Anna. "We're not *not* friends," she pointed out. "Maybe she just thinks I'm cool."

"If you say so." Dory shrugged and handed the note back, then took another bite of her sandwich.

What do you know about cool, anyway? Anna wanted to snap. *You've had the same haircut since third grade.* And *you have a blob of mayonnaise on your cheek.* Dory was definitely not the final authority on cool.

"Just forget it." Anna folded up the note and put it back in her pocket.

Dory absently rubbed her knuckles against her left collarbone. When Dory and Anna were little, Dory had fallen down the stairs at Anna's house and broken her collarbone, and there was still a visible bump where it had grown together unevenly. Dory was in the habit of rubbing this spot when she was thinking hard about something.

"Why do you think she wants to meet you in the old girls' bathroom?" she asked, clearly not ready to forget it.

Anna had wondered the same thing. The old girls' bathroom was located in a hallway between the main school building and the new gym. Not many people used it because it was dark and windowless; there were bigger, nicer bathrooms in the girls' locker room. Also, there were weird rumors about the old bathroom. Some kids swore it was haunted.

Anna had never heard any proof that the rumors were true, but the bathroom gave her the creeps all the same. She often found herself walking extra fast when she had to go by it. But she didn't want to admit to Dory that she was afraid.

"Probably because it's private," she said with a shrug. "Can we just forget it now?"

"Sure, whatever," said Dory. "Hey, so I've been thinking about our Halloween costume, and I've got it: toothbrush and toothpaste."

Anna and Dory always made their Halloween costumes together. In fact, Anna couldn't remember a Halloween where she hadn't dressed up with Dory.

Over the years they'd been fairy princesses, two black cats, M&M'S, twin witches, and a two-headed monster.

But a toothbrush and toothpaste? Anna raised her eyebrows. "Explain, please?"

"I got the idea when I was at the hardware store with my dad," Dory said. "See, one of us gets a scrub brush and wears it on the side of her head like toothbrush bristles. And the other one can wear a lampshade on her head — that's the toothpaste cap." Dory beamed, clearly pleased with her idea.

But Anna wrinkled her nose. "Dory, we're going to a Halloween *dance*, remember? Who's going to want to dance with a girl wearing a scrub brush on her head?"

"Oh." Dory's face fell. "I didn't think of that."

Anna sighed to herself. Sometimes it seemed to her that Dory still thought they were in grade school, where you could dress up like a toothbrush and people would think it was cute. In fact, when it came right down to it, Dory hadn't changed a bit since fourth grade. She still wore her hair in barrettes, brought her lunch in Tupperware containers, and talked about her pet hamsters as if they were real people. She still collected *rocks*, for Pete's sake.

Anna often found herself wishing that Dory would make just a little more effort to be *cool*.

Anna glanced over at the table in the center of the cafeteria, where Jessamyn was sitting with her BFFs, Kima and Lauren. Jessamyn laughed at something one of them was saying, swiping a lock of glossy black hair out of her eyes with a casual gesture that seemed glamorous to Anna.

Right from the first day of school, it had been clear that Jessamyn was glamorous. Even though she'd been just as new as every other seventh grader, she had known where to sit, who to talk to, and how to dress. It was like Jessamyn had been *born* cool, Anna thought.

Anna realized Dory was saying something to her. "What?" she asked, shifting her gaze back to her friend.

"I said, if you want I can go with you. To meet Jessamyn after school today," Dory replied.

"Oh." Anna hesitated. Jessamyn's note hadn't said anything about bringing a friend. But she and Dory always did everything together. Maybe this was exactly what Dory needed. But on the other hand, what if Jessamyn decided not to let Anna into the club because of Dory?

As Anna went back and forth, the bell rang. She stood up and dumped her lunch tray into the trash while Dory stacked up her Tupperware containers.

"Okay," Anna decided at last. "I'd like it if you came with me."

Dory nodded. "Okay."

"By the way," Anna added. "You've got something here." She tapped the corner of her mouth.

Dory grabbed a napkin and swiped away the offending blob of mayonnaise. Then she grinned. "Thanks, Anna."

At 3:09 P.M., Anna stood by her locker, nervously combing her fingers through her bangs. She had dark brown hair that she wore every day in two thick braids. The braids were something Anna was trying out. She'd read in a teen beauty magazine that every girl should have a signature look, whether it was a sharp haircut or a special color. At the start of seventh grade, the braids had seemed cute and sassy, something to make her stand out.

But now, gazing at herself in the mirror on her locker door, Anna wasn't so sure. She wished she had long, swishable hair like Jessamyn. She considered undoing the braids, decided it would take too long, and instead tried sweeping her bangs away from her face with the graceful gesture she'd seen Jessamyn use. They just fell back into her eyes.

Anna sighed. Her brown eyes gazed back at her from the mirror, full of doubt.

Someone tapped her shoulder. Anna jumped, and spun around.

"Hey," said Dory. She had on her backpack, which sagged with homework, and a yellow windbreaker that was two sizes too big.

Anna eyed Dory's backpack, which she was wearing on both shoulders as usual. Nobody in junior high wore their backpack on both shoulders — at least, nobody cool did. Anna opened her mouth to say something, then decided against it. She was glad Dory was coming with her, after all.

"Ready?" Dory asked. Anna nodded.

They made their way down the stairs, then turned toward the gymnasium. Wilson was shaped like a squared-off U, with the cafeteria and gymnasium forming separate wings off the main building.

They stopped in front of the old girls' bathroom. Anna glanced at Dory one more time, took a deep breath, then pulled open the door.

The room was dark. "Um, hello?" Anna said.

"Come in," said a voice from somewhere in the darkness. "Close the door."

Anna and Dory stepped inside and let the door swing shut behind them. Because there were no windows, the room was almost completely black. The only light came from a crack under the door.

Anna gave a little yelp as a light came on, illuminating a frightening face. It took her a second to realize it was Jessamyn. She was standing against the far wall, holding a flashlight under her chin to light up her face in a spooky way. Anna could see two figures standing on either side of her. Kima and Lauren.

Jessamyn swung the beam onto Dory's face like a spotlight. "What's she doing here?" she asked Anna sharply.

"She — she's my friend. I told her she could come," Anna stuttered.

One of the other girls — Lauren, Anna thought — stepped forward. "She's not supposed to be here —"

Jessamyn cut her off. "That's all right. The more the merrier." Anna thought she heard a smile in her voice. But at once, she became serious again.

Swinging the flashlight beam onto Anna, she asked, "Do you know why you're here?"

The light was blinding. Anna held up a hand to shield her eyes. "The note. It said I was chosen. . . ."

"That's right," said Jessamyn. "You have been specially chosen by me to be part of a secret club. Do you accept?"

Anna was about to say yes, but before she could, Dory broke in. "What is the club, exactly?"

There was a pause, as if Jessamyn was deciding how to answer. "I can't tell you. All the members are sworn to secrecy. You have to join first. Are you in or are you out?"

"In," Anna said promptly. She nudged Dory, who, after a moment's hesitation echoed, "In."

"Good." Jessamyn nodded. "But first you must go through the initiation."

"Initiation?" Anna asked with a shiver. All the darkness and secrecy were starting to get to her. Why couldn't they just turn on the lights?

Kima spoke up. "To be in the club, you must pass a test. You must face the spirits."

"How do you do that?" Anna's voice came out in a squeak.

"You have to look into the mirror and call on them," Lauren said. "If they say so, you can be in the club." She paused then added dramatically, "But if they don't like you, they could kill you."

Anna gulped so loudly she was sure everyone in the room had heard.

"This is stupid!" Dory suddenly burst out.

Anna turned to her friend with a gasp. *Shut up, Dory!* she thought in horror. She was going to ruin everything!

Jessamyn swung the flashlight beam onto Dory, who blinked in the sudden light. "Are you afraid?" she asked coolly.

"No," Dory snapped. "I think you're playing some dumb game, and I'm not interested. Come on, Anna." She turned to leave.

But Anna didn't move. Hadn't she been longing for something like this — something exciting, something to set her apart from the rest of the kids at Wilson? She wasn't willing to give it up so quickly.

Dory made a noise of disbelief or frustration, Anna couldn't tell which. They heard her stumble as she groped for the door. Then it swung open and closed, and Dory was gone.

"Sure you don't want to follow your lame friend?" Jessamyn asked Anna.

"No," said Anna. "I'm ready."

Jessamyn led her over to the mirror and handed her the flashlight. She showed her how to hold it under her chin. Held at that angle, light carved Anna's face with eerie shadows.

"Now, look into the mirror and say, 'Spirit in the mirror, I call on thee, come tell us what is to be.'"

"Spirit in the mirror, I call on thee..." Anna repeated. Her voice sounded high and uncertain. Behind her, she heard someone giggle.

Suddenly, Anna felt a flicker of doubt. What if Dory was right? Was this all a game, just some big joke?

"Don't stop!" Jessamyn commanded. "Look into the mirror. Keep repeating it."

"Come tell us what is to be." Anna sensed movement in the darkness behind her. What were they *doing*?

She didn't have time to wonder . . . because something was happening in the mirror. Her reflection was *changing*.

A face was emerging from the mirror's depths, like a swimmer surfacing through water. Little by little, its features took shape. Anna's heart gave a leap of joyful recognition, followed by a stab of fear.

The flashlight fell from her hand. Anna swayed, clutching the edge of the sink for balance as the room swung around her.

Distantly, as if from miles away, she heard Lauren say, "Look at her. What's *wrong* with her?" Then everything went black.

Chapter Two

When Anna opened her eyes, she was lying on the bathroom floor. The overhead light was on. Dory's worried face was peering down at her.

"Are you okay?" Dory asked. Her voice sounded fuzzy, as if she was speaking through water.

Anna stared at her, trying to figure out what she was doing on the floor. Slowly, it started to come back to her. She'd been at the initiation, looking in the mirror and then . . . what? Had she fainted?

She tried to sit up, which made her head throb. Anna winced and put her hand to it, feeling a tender lump just above her temple.

"Don't get up yet," Dory said sternly, so Anna lay back down. There was something soft behind her head. Out of the corner of her eye, Anna caught a glimpse of a yellow sleeve. Dory's windbreaker.

"What happened?" she asked groggily.

"I was out in the hallway, and I heard this *thud*. Then all those girls came rushing out of the bathroom like their feet were on fire. I went in and saw you lying here. I thought you were *dead*." Dory's forehead puckered with concern. "I guess you fainted."

So she *had* fainted. Embarrassment flooded Anna. *I must have looked so stupid, falling on the floor like that,* she thought. She wondered how much Jessamyn and her friends had seen.

"They ran away?" she asked Dory, not sure whether to be relieved or hurt.

Dory nodded angrily. "They just left you lying there. Those jerks."

Fragments of what had happened still were coming back to Anna, like bits of a dream. Abruptly, she sat up, despite her throbbing head. "Dory, I saw something in the mirror!"

Dory gave her a sad look. "It was just a joke, Anna. They were pranking you."

"No, really! I saw a face! It came out of the mirror. It was . . ." Anna put her hands to her head, trying to clear away the cobwebs that were clouding her thoughts. "I can't remember exactly, but I know I saw it."

Dory was silent for a moment, and the look in her eyes made Anna go cold. "Anna, I found this in a corner," Dory said finally. She held up a can of shaving cream. "It was all just a trick. I think they were planning to ambush you, to give you a big scare. But then you fainted, and I guess you scared them instead."

Anna was silent, burning with anger and shame. She wanted to tell Dory to stop lying, but she couldn't — because she knew Dory was right. It had all been a prank, and Anna had stupidly fallen for it.

She cast a furious glance at Dory, waiting for her to say, "I told you so." *But she doesn't even need to say it,* Anna thought bitterly. *It's written all over her face.*

Anna struggled to her feet, even though the movement made her head swim. Dory put a hand on her arm to steady her. "Are you sure you're okay? Maybe we should call your mom —"

"I'm *fine*, Dory," Anna snapped, shaking off her arm. "Just leave me alone!"

She turned on her heel and stormed out of the room.

Out in the hallway, her tears started to flow. *How could I have been so stupid?* She'd been so desperate to be accepted that she'd only made a fool of herself. Jessamyn and her crew were probably somewhere laughing their heads off right now. The thought made Anna sick.

She hurried toward the exit, swiping at the tears with the edge of her sleeve. The last bell had long since rung, and the other students were gone. She was halfway to the main doors when she heard footsteps echoing in the hall close behind her.

"Dory, I told you, leave me alone!" Anna cried, spinning around.

But there was no one there. The hallway was empty.

"I was just starting to wonder where you were," Anna's mother said as Anna came through the door later that afternoon.

Mrs. Dipalo was standing at the kitchen sink, still dressed in her nurse's uniform. Canned tomatoes and a box of spaghetti sat out on the counter, and a pot of water was starting to boil on the stove.

"I was over at Dory's," Anna lied. In truth, she'd been walking around for hours, too upset to go home. Now she kept her eyes to the ground. She didn't want her mother to see she'd been crying.

Her mother sighed heavily. "You know I like you to call me when you're going to be late."

"I guess I lost track of the time," Anna mumbled. She edged around her mother and headed for the door.

Her mother looked up from the lettuce she was rinsing. "Honey, you okay?"

Anna pretended not to hear. She escaped the kitchen and slowly climbed the stairs to her room. Shutting the door, she lay down on her bed, curled up on her side. She ran her fingers over the sore bump on her head, feeling sick and angry all over again.

Why me? she asked herself. Why had Jessamyn picked her to taunt, out of all the kids at school? Anna knew she wasn't the coolest kid at Wilson, but she wasn't the biggest nerd, either.

Was she?

Anna considered this carefully. There were lots of cliques at school, but Anna really didn't fall into any of them. It had always been just her and Dory, best friends ever since kindergarten. When they started middle school, it was almost like nothing had changed.

But things have *changed,* Anna thought. Middle school wasn't anything like grade school. At Wilson things *mattered* — like what you wore and what you said and where you sat in the cafeteria at lunchtime. And who you hung out with.

The more Anna thought about what had happened, the more it was Dory she felt angry with. When Dory had said, "But why would Jessamyn want *you* to join a club?" Anna was sure there had been a sneer in her voice. And that pitying look Dory had given her when it turned out she'd been right all along — ooh! That really burned her up!

Anna's brain went around and around in these thoughts until she was all worn out. At some point she heard the phone ring. When her father knocked on the door to say Dory was calling, she pretended to be asleep. Later, when he came to tell her dinner was ready, she really *was* asleep. She was barely aware of him taking off her shoes and turning out the light before she dozed off for good.

Chapter Three

"I had a great idea this morning!" Dory said the next day as she and Anna took their seats in their fourth-period science class. "The sun and the moon."

"What are you talking about?" Anna grumbled. All morning she had been acting cold toward Dory. But, much to her irritation, Dory hadn't seemed to notice.

"Our Halloween costume," Dory said. "We can be the sun and the moon. We'll paint our faces gold and silver and wear colors to look like the daytime and nighttime sky. It will be easy!"

"Don't you think we're getting a little old for all that? Dressing up in stupid matching costumes?" Anna said harshly. She didn't really think the sun and moon idea was stupid, but she was in a rotten mood, and it just came out.

Dory blinked. Finally, she seemed to notice that something was wrong. "Are you mad at me or something?" she asked Anna.

Instead of replying, Anna turned her head and looked out the window. It was a warm, sunny day — a last brilliant burst of Indian summer — and Anna longed to be outside. Or anywhere else, for that matter.

That morning, another note had landed on her desk in English class. Anna had unfolded it to see Jessamyn's neat, even handwriting.

> You are a loser.
> If you tell anyone you will be sorry.

Anna hadn't showed the note to Dory this time. She'd shoved it into the back of her English book and stared straight ahead, making her face into a mask. She hadn't wanted to give Jessamyn the satisfaction of seeing her upset.

But all morning tears kept pricking at the backs of her eyes. It was the "loser" part that hurt most.

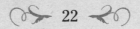

Anna knew there was no one in the world she'd ever be able to tell that to. She felt completely alone.

She was so caught up in her thoughts, she barely noticed when Mr. Cooper, the science teacher, began to pass out scissors, rubber gloves, aprons, and safety goggles. So when a metal tray with a dead frog in it landed on her lab table, Anna jumped back in alarm.

"What's going on?" she asked Dory.

"Weren't you listening?" said Dory. "We're dissecting frogs in class this week."

Anna and Dory gazed down at the stiff, rubbery body of their science experiment. Up at the front of the room, Mr. Cooper was explaining how to pin the frog down so they could cut it open. Anna felt her stomach heave.

Around them, the other students had started to get to work. But neither Dory nor Anna could get up the nerve to touch the frog.

Dory's small face looked as white as a sheet of paper. "You know more about this stuff than I do," she told Anna. "Your mom works in a hospital."

"My mom works with people, not frogs," Anna retorted. "Why don't you do it? You're the one who likes science, with your rock collection and everything."

"Those are rocks," Dory replied. "This is a *dead frog.*"

Mr. Cooper was strolling around the room, looking at everyone's work. He stopped next to Anna's table. "What's going on here, girls? Why are you just standing around?"

"Um . . ." Anna and Dory exchanged glances.

"Hey, Mr. C.!" a boy called from the next lab table over.

To Anna's relief, the teacher turned. "Yes, Benny?"

"Yo, I don't think it's fair," said Benny.

The teacher looked at him patiently. "What isn't fair?"

"That everybody should have to dissect frogs," Benny replied. "I mean, it's pretty nasty. And, you know, how does this prepare us for life? Unless we all grow up to be frog butchers."

This remark caused snickers. "Yeah, I got some frog legs cheap over here. Who wants a frog steak?" a boy at another table shouted out.

Around them, kids were laughing. Dory rolled her eyes. "Benny Riveras is such a smart aleck," she murmured to Anna.

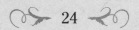

Benny might have been a smart aleck, Anna thought, but he was awfully cute, with his thick black hair and his long eyelashes.

"You don't *have* to dissect the frog, Benny," Mr. Cooper told him, ignoring his last comment. "If you object on the grounds that it's, as you say, 'nasty,' you can write a paper instead."

"A paper?" Benny asked skeptically.

Mr. Cooper nodded. "A two-page paper explaining the digestive and circulatory systems of an amphibian."

That was enough to shut Benny up. He glanced over at Anna and shrugged as if to say, "What can you do?" For the first time that morning, Anna smiled.

"Mr. Cooper, can anyone write the paper?" Dory asked suddenly.

"Well, yes," said the teacher, sounding surprised. Clearly, he wasn't used to anyone choosing this option. "You will need to cite at least three different sources. You can't just copy from the encyclopedia," he added, as if he thought that might change her mind.

But Dory didn't hesitate. "I'll take the paper," she said quickly.

"All right then." The teacher nodded. "I'll get you a pass for the library."

"Are you crazy?" Benny said to Dory as the teacher went to write out the pass. "He said *two whole* pages. You must really love homework."

Dory ignored him. "Tell Mr. Cooper you want to write the paper, too," she urged Anna.

Anna hesitated. Out of the corner of her eye, she noticed Benny watching her.

"I'm staying," Anna decided. After all, what kind of nerd would choose to write a paper when she didn't have to?

But Dory didn't hear her. She was waving at the teacher, trying to get his attention. "Mr. Cooper, Anna needs a library pass, too!" she called out.

"I *don't* want a library pass. I don't want to write the paper." Anna slammed her hand down in frustration. It caught the edge of the metal tray, flipping the frog onto the table. Dory jumped back with a little gasp.

"Geez, Anna, it's already dead. You don't have to kill it," Benny said, laughing.

"Here's your pass, Dory," Mr. Cooper said, coming back to their table.

Dory took the pass and headed for the door,

casting a bewildered glance over her shoulder at Anna. Then the door closed behind her with a soft click. *So long, sucker!* Anna thought.

But her small victory was short-lived. As she turned back to the table, she realized she still had a frog to dissect. And now she was going to have to do it alone.

Toughen up! Anna told herself. She was never going to make it through junior high if she kept acting like such a wimp.

Anna gritted her teeth. She picked up the knife.

As she leaned toward the frog, the room began to spin. There was a chemical smell in the air, and her vision started to tunnel.

"Mr. Cooper, Anna looks sick!" Benny called to the teacher.

The teacher took one look at her and ordered, "Go to the nurse's office!" Anna didn't need to be told twice. She dropped the knife and bolted from the room.

Out in the hallway, she stopped and leaned against a row of lockers. She closed her eyes and took several deep breaths. The metal lockers felt cool against her skin, and after a few moments she started to feel better.

"Escaped, huh?" said a voice in front of her.

Anna's eyes flew open. A girl she'd never seen before was standing in the hallway, watching her. *Where did she come from?* Anna wondered. She hadn't heard anyone approach. It was as if the girl had appeared out of thin air.

"What?" Anna asked, startled.

"You blowing off class?" The girl had a pale face half-hidden behind a tangle of long dark hair. She was wearing skinny jeans and a black hooded sweatshirt. Her hands were shoved into the deep front pockets.

She came closer. "Don't you talk?"

Anna stared. The girl had silver eyes.

No, not quite silver, Anna thought, looking closer. They were actually a pale shade of blue-gray, as cold and flat as metal discs.

"I'm not *ditching*, if that's what you mean," she said, finding her voice. "I got sick in class."

"School makes me sick, too." The girl cocked her head. The gesture was so familiar that Anna couldn't help feeling she'd met her somewhere before. "So, you want to get out of here?"

"What?" Again, Anna was startled.

"'What? What?'" the girl mimicked, but she didn't sound mean. "Is that all you say? I asked if you want to get out of here. You know, *ditch*."

Anna couldn't believe she was having this conversation with a total stranger. Clearly, the girl was nuts. But something — curiosity, maybe — kept Anna from walking away. "We can't leave," she said. "It's against the rules."

"Your teacher thinks you're in the nurse's office, and the nurse won't know one way or the other," the girl pointed out.

It dawned on Anna that she was right. She could walk right out, and no one would be any wiser. "But what about you?" she asked.

The girl smiled, and once again Anna was struck by the feeling she knew her. "Don't worry about me. I never get in trouble," the girl said. Without waiting for Anna, she turned and started toward the exit.

"Wait! What's your name?" Anna asked, hurrying to catch up with her.

The girl gave her a strange look. "Emma," she said, as if it was obvious, and pushed open the door.

The minute she stepped outside, Anna felt better. The fresh air washed away the last of her queasiness, and the sunlight warmed her clammy skin.

"So, where are we going?" Anna asked when they were a block or so from school.

"Wherever we want," Emma replied.

They continued down the street. At first, Anna was too nervous to enjoy herself. She was afraid she would run into someone she knew, one of her parents' friends maybe, who would ask why she wasn't in school. But the people they passed hurried by without giving them a second glance, and gradually Anna relaxed. She had never before in her life skipped school. The feeling of freedom was new and thrilling.

Not far from the school, they came to a little park, with a few benches, an old slide and swing set, and several pigeons. At 10:45 in the morning, it was empty.

"Hey, I've been here before!" Anna said. "I used to come here when I was a little kid. I forgot about this place."

She made a beeline over to the swing set and sat down on a swing. Emma took the swing next to hers.

"So, are you new at Wilson?" Anna asked as she gently rocked back and forth.

Emma nodded. "You could say that."

"I don't think I've seen you in the cafeteria. Who do you sit with?"

Emma shrugged in a way that could either have meant she had lots of different friends, or that she didn't care to have any. "Who are *your* friends?" she asked, fixing Anna with those strange silver eyes.

A chill ran across Anna's skin, as if a cloud had crossed the sun. She glanced up at the sky, but it was clear and blue. Emma was still looking at her, waiting for an answer.

"Well . . . Dory," Anna replied. "Dory Welch. She's my best friend, I guess."

Emma raised her eyebrows. "You guess?"

Anna sighed and kicked at the ground beneath the swing. "I don't know . . . lately, she kind of bugs me.

She thinks she's so smart," Anna complained, remembering the *I-told-you-so* look on Dory's face the day before. "She thinks she knows everything. But she doesn't. She doesn't get junior high at all." She wasn't sure why she was telling a stranger this. But Emma was listening with interest.

"And she's a total klutz," Anna said, warming up to her subject. "She's always tripping over stuff. And she's kind of a wimp. Like today, she chose to write a paper instead of dissecting a frog in science class. Can you believe that? A *two-page* paper."

"It doesn't sound like she's really your friend," Emma pointed out.

"Yeah. No. I don't know." Anna shook her head. "Maybe I just need a break from Dory right now."

Emma smiled in reply and began to swing.

Anna began to swing, too, pumping her feet hard to try to catch up with Emma. Back and forth they went, climbing higher and higher, until they were swinging so high that the chains went slack at the top of each arc, then snapped taut again as they swung down.

"Now jump!" Emma cried suddenly, and a second later she was sailing through the air.

Anna let go, too. Her stomach dropped as her heart soared. She was flying!

She landed feet-first in the bark around the swing set, then dropped to her knees and rolled to one side. Emma was lying on the ground, too. They both started to laugh.

"I've never done that before," Anna admitted. "I've never had the nerve."

"Stick with me," Emma said. "You'll be surprised what you can do."

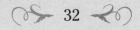

"You know, I keep feeling like I've met you some-where before," Anna said. "Isn't that funny? What's your last name?"

"Diablo," Emma replied. "'Cause I'm devilish. You'd better watch out." She wiggled her eyebrows wickedly, which set them off laughing again.

"Hey!" Anna said suddenly, noticing a flash of silver on Emma's finger. "Let me see your ring."

Emma stretched out her left hand. The ring on her pinky finger was silver, and set with a fire opal. "Do you like it?"

"You're not going to believe this, but I had one just like it when I was a kid. It was my favorite thing. I don't know what happened to it. I lost it, I guess." She admired the ring, twisting it so the opal glimmered in the sunlight. "Where did you get it?"

"An old friend gave it to me," Emma replied.

Anna shook her head. "What a crazy coincidence."

They swung on the swings for a while longer, tipping their heads back to admire the deep blue sky. Finally, Anna checked her watch. "We'd better get back. Fourth period is almost over."

"But it's lunchtime now," Emma pointed out. "Why go back? Nobody will miss us."

With the lunch money in her pocket, Anna bought a sandwich in a little deli across the street from the park. They split it, eating on a park bench, and talked. They discovered that they both hated pickles; they both liked Coke, root beer, and 7UP (in that order); and blue was their favorite color (though Anna liked light blue and Emma preferred dark). By the time they started back to school, Anna felt like she'd known Emma her whole life.

On the way back, they pretended to be spies, ducking behind bushes and peering around corners as they sneaked into the school yard. Anna was giggling hysterically by the time she made it to her locker. She knew one thing for certain: Emma was destined to be her friend.

"Where were you at lunchtime?" Dory asked Anna on the bus ride home from school that day.

"I was in the library. I forgot that I had a Spanish quiz, so I had to study." The lie slipped out so easily, Anna didn't even have to think about it.

"You could have told me." Dory sounded miffed. "I saved you a seat."

"Sorry," Anna said. "I guess I was so worried about the test I forgot. You know how it is."

She looked out the window, pretending to be lost in thought so Dory wouldn't ask more questions. She wasn't quite sure why, but she felt the need to keep her lunch with Emma a secret. It reminded her of the time she'd found a silver dollar on the sidewalk and hadn't told anyone about it. She had walked around with it in her pocket for weeks, just enjoying the feeling of having it there.

To Anna, Emma felt a bit like that silver dollar. Like a secret treasure that she had discovered and wasn't ready to share. Not just yet.

Chapter Four

Anna didn't see Emma again until the following day, on her way back from science class. That day, Mr. Cooper had moved Anna to Benny's lab table, and the two of them had agreed that Benny would do the dissection work while Anna took notes. He'd made jokes the whole time, and Anna had been so busy laughing that she'd hardly had time to get grossed out.

Anna was humming happily to herself when she rounded a corner and saw Emma standing at a locker. Her head was down, and she was fiddling with the combination.

"Hey!" Anna said, striding over to her. "I didn't know your locker was here. Mine's just around the corner." She was surprised she hadn't noticed Emma there before.

"This stupid thing," Emma snarled, still twirling the lock. "I can't get it open." She spun the combination one more time then gave the locker door a hard kick.

"My locker sticks sometimes, too," said Anna. "Want me to give it a try?"

Emma shoved her hands in her pockets and considered the lock. She was wearing the same black sweatshirt she'd had on the day before, but for some reason it looked bulkier. "Nah, forget it." She turned to Anna, her face brightening. "You're not doing anything for lunch, are you? Let's go somewhere."

"You mean, off campus?" Anna asked carefully. She'd had fun the day before, but she knew they were lucky they hadn't been caught. She wasn't sure she was ready to risk it again.

"No, it's not 'off campus,'" Emma mimicked with a smirk. She plucked at Anna's sleeve. "Come on, Miss Goody Two-shoes. It'll be fun."

Why not? Anna thought. An adventure with Emma sounded better than another dreary lunch in the cafeteria.

She followed Emma to the main stairway that led to the upper floors. The bell for lunch had already rung, and kids were streaming down the stairs, headed for the cafeteria. As she struggled against the tide, Anna felt like a salmon she'd once seen in a nature video, fighting its way upstream.

By the time they got to the third floor, the hallways were mostly empty. Emma glanced around surreptitiously, then darted into the girls' bathroom.

The bathroom? This wasn't quite the adventure Anna had been expecting. "You know, we didn't have to come all the way up here," she told Emma. "There's a bathroom on every floor."

Emma didn't reply. She was checking under the door of each stall. Finally, satisfied that they were alone, she went over to the frosted-glass window and tugged at the sash. The frame was sticky with paint, and she had to pull it a few times to get it open.

"After you." Emma gestured at the open window.

Anna was too stunned to reply. Did Emma expect her to *jump*?

"Fine," Emma said, with an impatient sigh. "I'll go first." Before Anna could say anything, she wriggled through the window and disappeared.

Anna gasped and raced over to look out. She was relieved to see that the window opened onto a fire escape. A set of narrow metal steps hugged the side of the building down to the first floor. But . . . where was Emma?

Anna heard a noise overhead. Twisting around, she saw Emma clambering up a rusted old ladder that was bolted to the side of the building.

"Better hurry," Emma called down to her. "Lunch is only forty minutes."

Anna gulped. She looked down again. Two stories below were the courtyard and basketball courts, both paved in blacktop. If she fell, there wouldn't be so much as an inch of grass to keep her head from smashing open like a watermelon.

She looked back up toward the roof and saw Emma's sneakers disappear over the edge.

Anna took a deep breath then hoisted herself out the window. As an afterthought she lowered it, just in case anyone came into the bathroom. Then she turned to the ladder.

The first rung was over her head. Anna pulled herself up by her arms, her feet scrabbling for purchase on the brick wall. When she managed to get onto the ladder, she clung there for a moment, shaking. Her hands were gripping the rungs so tightly she didn't see how she could possibly move them.

This is crazy, she thought. *I could get killed! Or worse — I could get detention!*

Emma's head popped over the side of the roof, her hair hanging down on either side of her face. Anna suddenly had a crazy vision of Emma pulling her up by her hair, like Rapunzel.

"Hurry. It's awesome up here," Emma said.

Anna took a deep breath. Slowly, she pried one hand off and quickly grasped the rung above. Then the other hand. Then one foot. And the other foot.

She worried that someone might spot her from below, but the ladder was hidden from the court- yard by an edge of the building that jutted out. Only someone standing directly below would have been able to see her.

Just keep going. Anna told herself. *Hand. Hand. Foot. Foot. Don't look down!*

Slowly, in this way, she made it to the roof. At the top of the ladder, Emma grasped her hands and pulled her over the edge.

The roof was surrounded by a low wall, and Anna leaned against it, gasping. "That . . . was . . . *the scariest thing I've ever done!"*

"But worth it. Take a look." Emma pointed behind Anna.

Anna turned around and sucked in her breath. The entire school yard spread out below them. They could see kids eating lunch at the outdoor tables and scrimmaging on the basketball courts. Beyond, the roofs of neighboring houses seemed to float in a sea of orange-and-gold-tipped trees. Farther still, Anna could see a glimmer of blue in the distance — the river that ran through town.

"Wow!" Anna breathed. "You can see the whole world from up here. How did you know about this?"

"It wasn't that hard to figure out," Emma told her. "I noticed the fire escape and just followed it all the way up. Look" — she pointed to one of the tables in the courtyard — "it's the Jackals."

Anna followed her finger and realized she was pointing at Jessamyn and her friends. "Jackals?"

"JKL. Jessamyn, Kima, Lauren," Emma explained. "They're vicious, and they travel in a pack, so I call them the Jackals."

"Jackals!" Anna howled. "That's perfect." She was both surprised and relieved to know that Emma didn't like Jessamyn. After all, practically everyone else at school did.

"Can I tell you a secret?" Anna asked, suddenly feeling she could confide in her new friend. She told Emma about Jessamyn's note, and explained how the other girls had tricked her into the old girls' bathroom so they could humiliate her. Anna left out the part about how much she'd once hoped to be like them.

Emma's eyes flashed with anger. "She's just trying to intimidate you. You can't let her."

"What can I do?" Anna said.

"We should get her back!" Emma declared.

"Yeah, right. That'll work," Anna said sarcastically. "She'd just turn the whole school against me." She sighed and looked down at the courtyard again. "Sometimes I hate this school. Nobody really cares to find out who you really are. You're either popular . . . or you don't exist."

"Like you're invisible?" said Emma.

"Yeah," Anna nodded.

"I know how that feels," Emma replied grimly. Anna waited for her to explain, but Emma scowled and fell silent.

Just then, Anna's stomach growled loudly. She put a hand on it and giggled, embarrassed. "I guess I'm hungry. I wish we had lunch."

"I almost forgot!" Emma cried, her expression brightening. She reached into the deep front pockets of her sweatshirt and began to pull out snacks. A snack-size bag of corn chips, a chocolate bar, sunflower seeds, bubblegum . . .

Anna's eyes widened. "You've got a whole convenience store in there!"

Emma shrugged. "So? I like junk food." She unzipped her sweatshirt and laid it on the roof like a picnic blanket, then spread out the snacks on top of it.

They spent the rest of the lunch period feasting on junk food and spying on the kids in the school yard below. Anna didn't see Dory, and she wondered if she had spent another day sitting alone in the cafeteria.

"Last chip?" Emma asked, interrupting her thoughts. She held out the bag.

As Anna took it, a breeze suddenly yanked the bag from her hand and sent it floating over the edge of the roof. Emma turned to Anna, her eyes wide. "I know how we can get the Jackals back! And they'll never even know who did it."

"How?" Anna asked.

"Meet me here same time tomorrow," Emma told her. She smiled her devilish smile, adding, "And bring a bottle of ketchup."

Chapter Five

When Anna climbed up the ladder the next day at lunch, Emma was already on the roof. She was sitting with her legs crossed and her eyes closed, as peaceful as a statue. Anna had the funny feeling that Emma had been there for hours, just waiting for her.

As if she felt Anna watching, Emma opened her eyes. "Did you bring it?" she asked.

Anna clambered over the edge of the roof and pulled the bottle of ketchup from her backpack. "I almost didn't get it. I thought my parents were never going to leave the kitchen this morning."

Emma fumbled in the pocket of her sweatshirt and pulled out a small package of balloons. Suddenly, Anna understood Emma's plan.

"You're kidding," she said.

"I'm not kidding at all," Emma replied, her expression dead serious.

"We can't do it. It's too . . . evil," Anna said.

"Oh, please." Emma rolled her eyes. "Think of who we're talking about. If you looked up *evil* in the dictionary, you'd find Jessamyn's name."

The ketchup was in a squeeze bottle, which made filling the balloons easier. Unfortunately, the bottle was only half full. In the end, they only had enough ketchup to fill three small balloons.

"Well, we have one for each Jackal. We just can't miss," Emma said, weighing a ketchup-filled balloon in her hand.

They went over to the edge of the roof and peered down. Plenty of kids were eating at the outdoor tables and milling around in the courtyard below. But there was no sign of the Jackals.

"What if they don't come outside today?" Anna asked.

"Then there's always tomorrow," Emma said. She paused then added, "But I hope we get a shot at them today. I noticed Jessamyn happens to be wearing white."

They waited for several minutes, splitting the

peanut butter sandwich Anna had brought in her backpack. Lunch was almost over when the Jackals finally emerged from the cafeteria.

"On your mark," Emma said.

"But they're all the way over on the other side of the courtyard!" Anna wailed. "We'll never hit them."

"Patience." Emma's gaze never wavered from the scene below.

They watched as the Jackals strolled around the courtyard. As usual, Jessamyn walked in the center of the pack. As Emma had mentioned, she had on a pair of white jeans along with a turquoise top. Her glossy hair was piled up in a ponytail on top of her head. Just seeing Jessamyn made Anna's blood boil, and her fingers tightened on the balloon. But the Jackals weren't coming anywhere close to the edge of the roof.

Anna's legs were beginning to cramp from crouching for so long. "Let's forget it," she said. "We'll try again tomorrow. . . ."

Her voice trailed off as she caught sight of Dory. She was sitting alone at one of the outdoor tables, watching a pickup game of basketball with an empty expression on her face.

Anna knew that her old friend had zero interest in sports. *She's pretending to watch the game,* she realized. *She doesn't have anyone else to sit with.* Anna was surprised at how detached she felt, watching this scene, almost as if Dory were a stranger.

"Anna! Now!" Emma's urgent cry broke through her thoughts. *"Now!"*

Anna barely had time to register that Jessamyn was standing below them before her hand opened and the ketchup-filled balloon was plummeting through the air toward its target.

A second later, a chorus of horrified squeals rang out from the courtyard below.

"Bull's-eye!" Emma crowed as they ducked below the edge of the roof.

"I wish I could have seen her face when she got hit," Anna said.

Just then, they heard Jessamyn's unmistakable squawk. "My white jeans! These are *designer*!"

"But," Anna added with a smile, "that was almost as good."

There was a lot of commotion at Wilson in the hours that followed. Several kids, including the entire

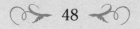 48

eighth grade debate team (who'd been meeting in a room right above the scene of the crime), were yanked into the dean's office for questioning. But no one thought to look on the roof, and Anna and Emma made it down without a hitch.

For the rest of the day, Anna was careful not to call attention to herself. In her afternoon classes, she discussed the attack with the same amazement as her classmates, but inside she was gloating. When she spied Jessamyn walking down the hall, dressed in her PE uniform and shooting murderous glares in every direction, Anna couldn't help giggling to herself.

From that point on, Anna and Emma were together every day. The fine weather continued, so they always met on the roof for lunch. Once she got over her fear of the ladder, Anna loved being up there. They ate and talked and spied on the kids in the courtyard below. One day, Emma asked Anna to teach her how to braid her hair, and after that she always wore her hair into two long pigtails, just like Anna's. Anna was flattered that Emma wanted to imitate her style.

They started hanging out together after school, too. Every day Emma would come up with new adventures for them. One day they climbed trees in the park, where they made up crazy birdcalls to startle people passing by. They scared one man so much that he dropped his briefcase, which popped open, sending papers flying. Anna almost fell out of the tree laughing at him. Another day, they took a bus to the Cineplex and snuck into a movie theater through the exit door, which had been left propped open.

As fun as Emma was, she could also be strangely secretive. Once, when Anna invited her to her house, Emma rolled her eyes and came up with something else for them to do instead. She never e-mailed or IMed, and when Anna asked for her cell phone number, she gave it with the warning, "But don't bother to call. I don't have any minutes on it, anyway." She never replied to the texts Anna sent her.

But these things hardly mattered to Anna. Emma was by far the most exciting person she'd ever met. Anna had never had a friend like her.

"What are we doing today?" Anna asked. It was a Thursday afternoon, a week after they'd started hanging out. Emma had asked her to meet her outside the art room after school.

"Stay here by the door, and tell me if anyone's coming," Emma instructed. She tried the knob then slipped into the art room.

Anna waited in the hallway, growing more impatient as the minutes ticked by. Finally, she cracked open the door and peeked inside to see what Emma was doing.

Emma was at the teacher's desk, digging through a lower drawer. Anna's heart skipped a beat. Messing around in a teacher's desk? What was Emma *thinking*?

A minute later, Emma emerged from the room with two cylindrical cans. "Put these in your backpack," she told Anna.

Anna eyed the cans. "Is that spray paint?"

"No, it's canned cheese," Emma sniped, rolling her eyes. "Yes, of course, it's spray paint. Now, hurry. Before someone comes."

"You stole it," Anna said accusingly.

"I *borrowed* it," Emma corrected.

"Fine, you 'borrowed' it. But why take it at all? Why don't we just buy some?"

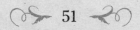

"Duh, you can't buy spray paint if you're a kid. Everyone knows that. In stores, they lock this stuff up like it's plutonium. I think they even make you show ID to buy it," Emma said. "Stop looking at me like that. It's just a couple cans."

"Then why don't *you* carry it?" Anna asked.

"Because someone *might* notice if I'm walking out of school with my arms full of spray paint," said Emma.

For the first time, Anna realized Emma didn't have a backpack. In fact, she'd never even seen Emma with any schoolbooks. *How does she do her homework?* Anna wondered suddenly.

"Look," Emma said, her face softening. "Tell you what. *I'll* carry the bag."

With a sigh, Anna unzipped her backpack. Emma put the two cans inside, then zipped it back up and swung it over one shoulder.

"Let's go!" she said.

Just as they started away from the art room, the janitor came around the corner, the keys on his belt jingling. Emma kept right on walking, her chin held high, but Anna glanced back over her shoulder. She saw the janitor step into the room where Emma had been just moments before. Anna felt her scalp tingle at how close they'd come to being caught.

Once they were on the sidewalk, Emma began walking quickly, like a soldier setting out on a mission. Anna wanted to ask where they were going, but Emma's mind seemed to be in another place, so she kept quiet.

They passed houses with pumpkins sitting on the front porch and Halloween decorations taped in the windows. Emma kept up a brisk pace, and sometimes Anna matched her stride exactly, so they were walking in lockstep. At those moments, it really did seem to Anna like they were soldiers — an army of two, just them against the world.

Gradually, the houses became more run-down. They saw row houses with peeling paint and yards full of unraked leaves. When the houses gave way to buildings, mostly warehouses, with empty lots in between, Anna knew they were getting close to the river.

"Where are we going?" she finally asked.

"Almost there," Emma said in reply.

They walked another block and came to an old brick building surrounded by a chain-link fence. Some of the windows were covered with plywood, while others were just gaping holes, like empty eye sockets in a skull. The building was clearly abandoned. Nearby, cars rushed past on the ramp leading up to the bridge that crossed the river into downtown.

Anna had seen this building before on car trips with her parents; seen it in the way you see things without really noticing them. It was just part of the landscape, an ugly blotch that her eye usually passed over in search of something more interesting.

Ignoring a NO TRESPASSING sign, Emma squeezed through a hole in the fence. Anna followed reluctantly. The ground around the building was littered with glass bottles, rusted beer cans, and cigarette butts — evidence that other people had been there. People Anna didn't necessarily want to run into.

When they got to the building, Emma set down the backpack and took out the cans of paint. Now Anna knew why they were there. The brick wall of the building was covered in graffiti.

"You said you felt invisible," Emma said, handing her a can of paint. "Now's your chance. Put your name where hundreds of people will see you every day." She swept an arm toward the cars buzzing past on their way to the bridge.

Anna's heart began to pound. She'd heard of kids being fined hundreds of dollars for getting caught tagging buildings. But now that she was standing there with the can of spray paint in her hand, the urge to write something was irresistible.

She studied the tags that were already there: scrawled names, goofy faces, initials in big bubble letters. *Spaz. MJ rules. GoGo.*

Anna uncapped the can and slowly shook it, listening to the bead inside rattle. After a second's hesitation, she wrote ANNA on the wall in big block letters.

She stepped back and giggled. She'd done it!

Emma nodded approvingly. She uncapped the other paint can and wrote EMMA in red next to Anna's name.

Emma shook the can again, hard, then continued to write, so now it read

ANNA + EMMA = BEST FRIENDS FOREVER!

Emma stepped back and stood next to Anna. They both stared at the words. Emma had written in such huge letters that it stood out from everything else on the wall. Anna felt a little thrill. No one could miss seeing their names now.

"It's permanent," Emma said in a thoughtful voice. "It can never be erased."

After that, they sat leaning against the wall, watching the traffic and the river flowing by below. The river water was gray and sludgy, and occasionally some bit of trash would come bobbing along. But it felt good to sit there with the warm sun on their faces.

"Why do you keep fiddling with that?" Emma asked.

Anna looked down and realized she was twisting her bracelet around and around on her wrist. It was a beaded friendship token Dory had made for her the year before. "I didn't even notice I was doing it," she said.

Emma grabbed Anna's wrist and examined the bracelet. "It's cool," she said. "I'll trade you for it."

Anna hesitated. It seemed wrong to give a friendship bracelet away, even if Dory wasn't her friend anymore. "It's just an old bracelet," she said. "It's not worth anything."

"Come on. I'll trade you for my ring," Emma said, holding out her pinky ring. The fire opal flashed in the sunlight. "We *are* best friends forever, right?"

This was too much for Anna to resist. She'd so wanted a friend like Emma. She undid the clasp on the bracelet and passed it over. *Dory will never know,* she thought. *And anyway, Emma's my best friend now.*

Anna slipped the ring onto her right pinky finger and admired it. She felt as if she'd found the old ring she'd lost as a kid.

A gust of cool wind blew off the river, ruffling Anna's bangs. Suddenly, she noticed how low the sun was in the sky. "I'd better get home," she said, hopping up. "If I'm late for dinner, my mom'll kill me."

Emma climbed to her feet, too. "Do you do everything your parents tell you?"

Anna shrugged. "I guess so. I mean, they're my *parents.*"

Emma mumbled something that sounded like, "You didn't used to." But her face was turned toward the river, and Anna couldn't really hear.

"What did you say?" she asked.

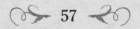

Emma turned back to her. "Nothing. Come on. Let's go."

They walked together back to school. "See you tomorrow?" Emma asked as they parted ways.

"Yup." Anna nodded. She watched as Emma walked away, her braids swinging behind her like two long chains.

Then she turned and set out for her own house, turning up her collar and shrugging her shoulders against the chill wind that had suddenly come up. Despite the cold, Anna felt warm with happiness. Emma Diablo, the coolest girl at school, was her best friend. Forever.

Chapter Six

"I haven't seen Dory around here in a while," Anna's mother remarked that evening.

They were in the kitchen, washing up after dinner. Anna rinsed a frying pan under running water and handed it to her mother. "Yeah, I guess we haven't been hanging out much," she replied carefully.

Anna's mother looked at her as she ran a dishcloth over the pan. She had eyes like Anna's — big and dark, with long eyelashes. "Did you two have a fight or something?"

"No, Mom," Anna huffed, blowing her bangs out of her eyes. It was the truth. She'd never actually had a fight with Dory. She'd just sort of stopped hanging out with her, without ever explaining why.

"It's not like I have to do everything with Dory," she added. "I have other friends, too, you know."

"Of course," her mother said lightly. "I just wondered, that's all."

"In fact, I made a new friend at school," Anna went on. "Her name is Emma."

"That's a pretty name." Mrs. Dipalo's lips curled in a tiny smile.

"What's so funny?" Anna asked.

"Oh, it just reminded me of something," her mother said as she dried a serving spoon. "You had an imaginary friend named Emma when you were little. Don't you remember?"

Anna shook her head.

"It was a long time ago, before Dory moved into the neighborhood. All the kids on our block were older, and I think you missed having someone to play with."

Mrs. Dipalo paused with the spoon in midair, remembering. "Although she was more like your partner in crime. You were always getting into trouble and blaming it on Emma. Like the time you poured juice on your father's laptop. Or the time you pulled the heads off all our neighbor's roses." She laughed. "That one I'll never forget. Mrs. Knox was furious. When I asked you why you did it, you said, 'I didn't do it, Mommy. Emma did!'"

"That's funny." Anna furrowed her brow. "I don't remember doing any of those things."

"Well, I'm not surprised. It was a long time ago," her mother said. "But I'll tell you, I was glad when Dory came along. We didn't hear too much about Emma after that."

As they finished up the dishes, Anna's mother seemed to be thinking about something.

"I'm glad you made a new friend, sweetie," she said, after a moment. "But don't forget the old saying."

"What saying?" asked Anna as she handed her the last pot to dry.

" 'Make new friends, but keep the old; one is silver and the other's gold.' "

Anna rolled her eyes. "Mom, that's *so* corny."

"Corny, maybe," her mother replied. "But true."

Anna unplugged the sink then dried her hands on a clean dishtowel. "Are we done here?"

Mrs. Dipalo looked around the clean kitchen. "I guess we are. You are released from duty."

"Good," said Anna. " 'Cause I've got homework."

By the time she'd climbed the stairs to her room, her mother's words had already faded from her mind. She was too busy thinking about the fun she'd had with Emma that day, and wondering what new adventures the next day would bring.

Now that she spent all her free time with Emma, Anna hardly ever saw Dory. The only class they shared was science, and since Anna had moved to Benny's lab table, they no longer talked there, either. If she saw Dory coming down the hall, she usually ducked the other way. Anna didn't like confrontation. If she could have, she would have gone on avoiding Dory forever.

But, as it happened, the very next day Dory caught her at her locker as Anna was putting her books away. "Hey, Anna!" Dory called, striding over.

Anna groaned inwardly. She glanced up and down the hall, wondering if she should pretend to have to rush off somewhere. But it was too late. Dory had already reached her.

"I haven't seen you for a while," Dory said a little too brightly. She was breathing fast, as if she'd hurried to get there. "Want to come over after school today? I'm working on a new video starring Hester and Harold. It's going to be *Romeo and Juliet.*"

Hester and Harold were Dory's pet hamsters. Dory loved to film movies with them in the lead roles. There was a time when Anna would have thought doing *Romeo and Juliet* with hamsters was a hilarious way to spend the afternoon. But that time was over since she'd met Emma.

"Sorry, I can't." Anna pretended to search for something in her notebook, hoping Dory would take the hint and leave.

But Dory just stood there. "Are you mad at me?" she asked suddenly, the brightness gone from her voice.

Anna sighed. "I just think," she mumbled, without quite looking Dory in the eye, "maybe we just shouldn't hang out anymore."

Dory stared at her. "Why not?"

At that moment, Anna caught sight of Emma coming toward them through the crowded hallway. *Thank goodness,* she thought. Anna smiled and waved to her. But although Emma seemed to glance in her direction, she walked past without stopping.

"Who are you waving at?" asked Dory, following her gaze.

"Emma," Anna replied distractedly. *What was that all about?* she wondered.

Dory's brow wrinkled. "Who's *Emma*?"

"My friend. She's right —" Anna broke off. Emma had disappeared.

"Well, maybe we could all hang out sometime." Dory tried a smile, but her voice quavered.

Stop being so pathetic! Anna wanted to shout. "Look," she said sharply. "I just don't think we have anything in common, Dory. Okay?"

Before Dory could reply, Anna slammed her locker shut and hurried away. She had to find Emma and make sure that nothing was wrong.

Anna looked for Emma by her locker, but she didn't find her there. She checked everywhere else she could think of, even going up to the third-floor bathroom to see if the window was open (the sign that Emma was on the roof), but it was shut tight and locked from the inside. Emma didn't seem to be in any of her usual places.

It wasn't until Anna had given up and was leaving school that she spotted Emma. She was standing at a maple tree in front of the school, leaning against its trunk. She made no move to greet Anna as she hurried up.

"I've been looking all over for you," Anna said. "Why didn't you say hi to me in the hall?"

"What were you and Dory talking about?" Emma asked coldly.

"Nothing!" Anna said. Was *that* what Emma was upset about? "She just wanted to know what I was doing after school."

"I thought you said she wasn't your friend anymore."

"She's not. We were just talking," Anna explained, confused. Why was Emma acting so strange?

Emma said nothing, but her eyes pierced Anna coldly. Anna shivered and tugged at the zipper of her windbreaker. After the long stretch of Indian summer, the weather had finally taken a turn. Now, heavy clouds filled the sky like piles of wet cotton, and the sharp smell of burning leaves hung in the air.

"We were just talking," Anna repeated. "Let's forget it, okay?" She tried a smile. "So, what should we do today? Want to go back down by the river? I think there's still some paint left. Or we could go to the park. . . ."

Emma pushed herself off the tree. "Not today. I have something to take care of."

Without any more explanation, she turned and walked away.

Saturday morning, Anna awoke to the sound of the phone ringing. She rolled over in bed and checked her clock. It was just after seven thirty. *Who would call so early on a Saturday?* she wondered with irritation.

Anna flopped back on her pillow and closed her eyes, but she couldn't go back to sleep. Finally, she climbed out of bed. She pulled on jeans and a sweater and went down to the kitchen.

Her mother was standing in the middle of the room holding the cordless phone. She had a funny look on her face. "That was Dory's mother on the phone," she told Anna.

"Oh, yeah?" said Anna. She got a box of cereal down from the cupboard and poured herself a bowl, then went to the refrigerator to get milk.

"Something happened at the Welches' house last night," Mrs. Dipalo said.

Anna paused with her hand on the refrigerator handle, waiting for her mom to go on.

"Their property was vandalized," her mother told her. "Someone wrote on the lawn in spray paint."

Anna's mouth fell open. "What did they write?" she asked.

Her mother cleared her throat, as if she wasn't quite comfortable saying it out loud. " 'Dorky Dory.' "

"That's awful!" *It had to have been the Jackals,* Anna thought. *They're getting back at her for walking out on their stupid trick. Poor Dory.*

"Do they know who did it?" she asked her mother, wondering if she should say something about Jessamyn.

Mrs. Dipalo's worried eyes burrowed into Anna's. "Dory says it was you."

"What?"

"Dory told her mother that she heard something in the middle of the night. She looked out the window and saw you running down the street."

"It's not true!" Anna exclaimed. "She's lying."

"Why would she say something like that?" her mother asked.

"She's just jealous because I've been hanging out with Emma. And now she's trying to get back at me." Anna yanked open the refrigerator door and grabbed the milk. "I can't believe she would say that! You believe me, right? You know I would never do something like that."

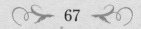

"That's what I told her mother." Mrs. Dipalo looked relieved. "I knew it couldn't have been you."

Anna sat down at the table to eat her cereal. She spooned it into her mouth, chewing furiously, but she didn't taste a thing. She was so mad she could hardly think straight.

The nerve of Dory, trying to get her in trouble like that! The sympathy Anna had felt for her just moments before had vanished.

When she'd finished eating, Anna prowled around the house, looking for something to do, but she was too worked up to focus on anything. Every time she thought about Dory, she felt angry all over again.

Finally, Anna put on her sneakers and her jacket, got her bike out of the garage, and pedaled the few blocks to Dory's house.

When she got close, she slowed down. Dory's older brother, Drew, was out front, mowing the lawn. He ran the mower back and forth across the grass, but Anna could see that it wasn't doing much good. The bright red letters DORKY DORY were still clearly visible in the green grass. It would be days, or even weeks, before they faded.

Anna rode past slowly, making sure to stay on the far side of the street so Drew wouldn't notice her. As she glanced up at the house, she thought she saw a curtain move, but no one appeared in the window.

Was it Dory? Anna wondered. She imagined Dory sulking behind the curtains, waiting for her to come up the front steps and apologize.

Well, she can wait for the rest of her life, because it's never going to happen! Anna thought, pedaling away. As far as she was concerned, her friendship with Dory was over. For good.

Chapter Seven

The rest of the weekend dragged by. Anna tried to call Emma several times, but she always got a message saying the number was disconnected. She figured Emma hadn't paid for her minutes again. With nothing else to do, Anna spent the weekend moping around the house and plotting what she'd say to Dory when she saw her at school on Monday.

But on Monday Anna didn't see Dory at her locker, and in science class, Dory's seat was empty.

"Did you hear about Dory? Or, I should say, 'Dorky Dory,'" Anna overheard someone say at the next table. It was Krystal, the biggest gossip in the seventh grade, gabbing to her lab partners as usual.

If Krystal was talking about Dory, Anna knew that meant everyone in school had heard about what had happened — or soon would. For as long as she was at Wilson, no one would ever say Dory's name again without adding "Dorky" to it.

Well, she deserves it, Anna fumed as she stared at Dory's empty seat. *Serves her right for trying to get me in trouble, the little backstabber.*

"Hey, hello out there." Benny waved his hand in front of her face. "Earth to Anna."

"Huh?" Anna blinked at him.

"Phew!" Benny feigned relief. "For a second there, I thought you'd donated your brain to science."

Anna giggled. Benny's jokes were kind of dumb, but they always made her laugh.

"So," he said, "are you going to help me on this experiment or what?"

Thoughts of Dory slipped from Anna's mind as she and Benny turned to their assignment.

To Anna's relief, they'd moved on from frog anatomy and now they were studying cells. That day, they were supposed to classify different cell drawings on a worksheet. But Benny wasn't being much help.

"This looks like a pepperoni pizza cell," he joked, pointing to one of the drawings. "And this is clearly a deep-dish sausage and onion cell."

Anna rolled her eyes. "Are you *hungry* by any chance?"

"Starving," said Benny. "I'd give anything for a slice right now."

"Well, try not to drool on the worksheet," Anna joked. "Lunch is in twenty minutes."

Benny made a face. "Who wants gross cafeteria pizza? I'm jonesing for Moxie."

Anna gave him a blank look.

"You don't know *Moxie*?" Benny looked shocked. "It's only, like, the best pizza on the *planet*. You do eat pizza, right?"

"Obviously," said Anna.

"You haven't *lived* unless you've had Moxie pizza," Benny told her. "I'm going there after school today. You should come."

Anna's smile froze. *Did Benny just ask me out?* she wondered.

Benny seemed just as surprised because he started to stammer. "Y-you don't have to. I mean, it's no big deal. I'm just going with a few of my friends and —"

"It sounds fun," Anna interrupted. "I'd like to come."

"Really? That's cool. Okay, so I'll see you there

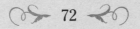 72

after school. Wow. Okay. Cool," Benny babbled. He seemed almost relieved when Mr. Cooper yelled at them to stop talking.

When the bell rang, Benny quickly scooped up his books. "Meet you there at three fifteen!" he told Anna, and rushed out of the room.

Anna slowly collected her things and floated out the door, humming to herself. She had a date with Benny!

Well, not a date, she reminded herself. *We're just hanging out with a bunch of kids. But I think maybe he likes me. Wait till I tell Emma!*

But when she did see Emma, moments later, Anna lost the nerve. Emma was leaning against Anna's locker, with her arms folded across her chest. "Where have you been?" she asked accusingly. "I've been waiting for you."

"I was in class." Anna was surprised at her friend's strange behavior. She seemed so cold and bossy lately.

"Whatever," Emma huffed. "Come on. I'm hungry. Let's go to lunch."

Anna glanced out the window, which was spattered with rain. "I guess the roof is out today. We'll have to eat in the cafeteria."

Emma gave her a look of disdain. "You mean, the barfeteria? No thanks. I've got a better idea. Let's go to the diner on Fifth Street."

"I can't," Anna said. "I don't have enough money." She had only a few dollars in her pocket, and she wanted to save them for Moxie. "Anyway, I brought my lunch today."

"Don't worry about the money. I've got us covered."

Anna opened her mouth to object, then changed her mind. She didn't think she'd win an argument with Emma.

Outside, the rain was slashing down. They pulled up their hoods and sprinted the few blocks to the diner. Even so, they were soaked when they came through the door.

A waitress walking past with a pot of coffee glanced at them and pursed her lips. She pointed to a booth in the corner near the door.

"Perfect," Emma said. She slid across the yellow vinyl seat, streaking it with rainwater.

After a moment, the waitress came over and dropped a single menu on their table. She had on thick blue eye shadow, and her curly hair was piled like a haystack on her head. "Something to drink?" she asked them tiredly.

Emma ordered coffee, and after a moment's hesitation Anna did, too. She never drank coffee, but it sounded sophisticated. Not to mention warm. She was shivering in her wet clothes.

The waitress sloshed coffee into two cups that were already on the table. Emma ordered a turkey sandwich for them to share. The waitress wrote their order down on a little pad, stuck her pen behind her ear, and shuffled off to the kitchen.

"Nice service," Emma said with a snort.

Anna didn't say anything. She'd just taken a sip of the hot, bitter coffee and scalded her tongue. She fanned her burning mouth with one hand and pushed the cup away with the other.

Emma leaned back in the booth, kicking her dirty sneakers up on the seat next to Anna. "Isn't this great? Way better than eating in that lame cafeteria."

Anna glanced around the room. There were a few people in business suits sitting at the counter, staring into space as they chewed their sandwiches. In the booth across from Anna, a lonely-looking old man was spooning cottage cheese into his mouth.

The diner didn't seem so great to Anna. At least at school, there were other kids.

"You know, maybe we should cool it for a while. Cutting school, I mean. We're going to get caught one of these days," she said.

Emma waved a hand as if that was of no concern. "So today, I was thinking we'd —"

Their conversation was interrupted by the arrival of the waitress, who plunked their food down, slapped a check on the table, and headed off to wait on some other customers.

"I can't hang out today," Anna said when she was gone. "I'm meeting Benny Riveras."

Emma was dumping packets of sugar into her coffee, but she glanced up sharply. "Benny? What for?"

Anna explained how Benny had invited her to Moxie for pizza. "You can come, too," she said quickly. "He said a bunch of kids are going."

"I can come, too? Gee, *thanks* for the invitation," Emma sneered sarcastically.

"I thought you'd be happy for me," Anna said, feeling hurt.

Emma made a face. "Happy that you're hanging out with that *twerp*?"

"Benny's not a twerp. He's nice. And funny. And I think he likes me." What was wrong with Emma? Why was she being so mean?

Emma shrugged. "Fine. Go hang out with him if you want. Just don't say I didn't warn you."

"What's that supposed to mean?" Anna asked. But Emma wouldn't explain.

Anna nibbled at her sandwich, but she didn't feel hungry. This lunch had turned out horribly. She just wanted it to be over.

But once she was done eating, Emma dawdled. She kept glancing over at the waitress. Anna had the feeling she was waiting for something.

When the waitress disappeared into the kitchen, Emma suddenly stood. "Let's go!" she hissed.

"You haven't paid the bill yet," Anna pointed out.

"Haven't you ever heard of dining and ditching?"

"But you said you were going to pay!" Anna couldn't believe what Emma was pulling.

"I said I had it taken care of," Emma said. "I didn't say I'd pay. I don't even have any money. Now come on, we have to go *now*." Without waiting for Anna, she dashed out the door.

Anna jumped up from the table so quickly she made the coffee cups rattle. A couple in the next booth looked up from their food. Halfway to the door, though, Anna stopped, frozen with indecision. She saw the kitchen door swing open and the waitress come out carrying a tray of food.

At the last second, Anna darted back to the table, pulled a few crumpled dollar bills from her pocket, and dropped them on top of the check. It wasn't enough to cover the bill. But it was all she had.

"Won't she come after us?" Anna gasped when she'd caught up with Emma.

"No way! Did you see that hairdo? She'd never risk getting it wet." Emma laughed nastily. "She was a horrible waitress. Did you notice how she only brought us one menu? We really got her back."

Anna didn't laugh along with her. All she could think about was how tired the waitress had looked. For the first time ever, hanging out with Emma didn't seem like that much fun.

Chapter Eight

That day, after her last class, Anna went by Emma's locker, hoping she might be able to convince her to come to Moxie after all. Emma wasn't there, so Anna lingered for a few minutes in case she showed up.

Just a few lockers down from Emma's, the Jackals were clustered around Jessamyn's locker, gossiping. When Jessamyn noticed Anna watching them, she narrowed her eyes, as if to say, *What are you looking at?* The other Jackals turned and looked at Anna.

With their eyes on her, Anna gave up on waiting for Emma and scurried away.

By the time she got to Moxie, the place was packed. Anna made her way past the tables of kids scarfing bread sticks and pizza slices. The air was full of the jangle of pinball machines and the smell of burnt pizza crust.

She found Benny in the back by the air hockey table. "Hey!" he exclaimed happily when she walked up. "I was worried you weren't coming. Anna, do you know Pete and Eamonn?"

His two friends glanced up and nodded, then went back to their air hockey game.

"They've been hogging the table," Benny said. "But I'm up next." He pointed to a little stack of quarters on the side of the table. "Want to get a slice while we're waiting?"

"That's okay . . . I'm not really hungry," Anna fibbed. She was ravenous, but she'd left what money she had at the diner.

"But you have to have a slice! It's Moxie!" Benny exclaimed. "Don't worry. I've got you covered."

Anna watched as Benny strode over to the counter. He chatted for a minute with a guy at the register and waved to someone in the kitchen. They both peered over the counter at Anna, who blushed.

Benny returned a few minutes later carrying a tray with pizza slices and two Cokes. He set it down on a wooden table plastered with bumper stickers.

"Dig in," Benny said as he picked up his slice.

Anna hesitated. "Were you . . . going to pay for it?" She didn't want to end up in another dine-and-ditch situation.

Benny waved a hand. "My aunt and uncle own this place. So I pretty much get to eat for free. My uncle's the guy in the back throwing the pizza dough. Go on." He nudged Anna. "It's best when it's really hot."

Anna relaxed and picked up her slice. Strings of molten cheese oozed off the sides. When she took a bite, the cheese burned the roof of her mouth, but she didn't care because the sauce was tangy and the crust was chewy. Benny was right. It was the best pizza she'd ever had.

While they ate, they laughed at the bumper stickers on the table. *Honk if you like Heron's Pretzels. Visualize Whirled Peas. What if the Hokey Pokey really IS what it's all about?* Anna had the feeling that Benny had probably read them all a hundred times before, but he still laughed every time she pointed out a funny one.

"That one's mine," Benny said, pointing to a sticker that read *Go Hounds! 2010 Junior Hockey League Champions.*

"You play hockey?" Anna asked. "I didn't know there was a team at school."

"There isn't," Benny told her. "I play in a club league. Two-time champs! Put 'er there!" He held up his hand so Anna could slap a high five.

"Practice starts next week for this season," Benny told her. "Man, I can't wait! Sometimes in the summer, when the ice rink shuts down, I ride my bike over anyway, just to imagine being out on the ice again." Benny glanced at Anna with an embarrassed smile. "I guess that sounds kind of dumb, huh?"

Anna smiled and shook her head. She'd been thinking how different Benny seemed. At school he was such a goofball. But when he was talking about hockey he sounded so sincere. *There are so many things about a person you can't tell just by looking at them,* she thought.

"Speaking of hockey," Benny said, glancing toward the air hockey table, "I think we're up."

"Uh-uh. No way," said Anna. "I'm not ready to go up against a professional."

Benny took her hand and pulled her to her feet. "Come on," he said. "Sometimes you just gotta be brave."

They played three rounds of air hockey. Benny goofed around a lot, trying to make shots behind his back, and he cheered whenever Anna scored a goal. After that, they played pinball and Anna beat him. She played his friend Eamonn and beat him, too. Even though Benny said he didn't like pinball, she could tell he was having a good time, because he kept calling "Rematch!" and putting more quarters in the machine.

By the time Anna remembered to call home it was after five o'clock. Benny listened with a sympathetic look on his face while she apologized to her mom half a dozen times for not calling sooner.

"I have to go home," Anna said when she'd hung up. "She's pretty mad. I promised her I'd get the bus right now."

"You're too late for the school bus. And the city bus will take forever," Benny said. "I'll give you a ride."

"Your uncle can give me a lift?" Anna asked, relieved.

"Who needs him? I've got my own wheels," Benny replied.

Anna gaped at him. "You have a *car*?"

Benny laughed. "Yeah, that's right. My Benz. Come on."

He said good-bye to his friends and led the way outside. In front of the building was a bike rack, with a beat-up mountain bike chained to it. "There she is. Benny's Benz," he said proudly.

Anna laughed. "But how are we both going to ride?" she asked.

Benny considered this. "You'll have to sit on the seat, and I'll stand on the pedals."

"Is this safe?" Anna asked, climbing onto the seat as Benny held it steady.

"Probably not," said Benny. "You should wear this." He handed her his bike helmet. Anna put it on and fastened the strap under her chin.

"That looks good on you," Benny said approvingly, and Anna felt her face get warm.

The sky was starting to turn pink as they set out for Anna's house. Anna tried to balance on the seat as gracefully as possible, but it wasn't easy. She had to hold her feet out to the sides to keep them from getting tangled in the spokes. There was nowhere for her to put her hands except on Benny's waist. Out of shyness, she held him there as lightly as possible as he pedaled them through the streets.

Despite how awkward it was, Anna thought it was the most romantic thing she'd ever done.

"There's my house," Benny said, nodding at a two-story white house. Anna craned her neck with particular interest as they passed it.

By the time they reached Anna's street, the sun had begun to set. It had stopped raining hours before, and now the sky was aflame with red and orange clouds.

"You'd better drop me off here," Anna said when they reached the corner. Benny braked, and she climbed off the bike. "Thanks for the ride."

"No problem." Benny stood there straddling the bike, looking as if he was waiting for something. They stared at each other for a moment. *In a movie, this is where we'd kiss,* Anna thought.

"Well, see you in school," she said finally. She turned and started for home.

"Anna, wait!" said Benny.

Anna stopped and looked back, her heart starting to pound.

"I need my helmet," Benny said.

"Oh! Duh." Anna walked back to him, laughing as she undid the chin strap. She could feel herself blushing, and she hoped Benny couldn't guess what had just been going through her head.

"See you tomorrow," Benny said. Then he turned around on his bike and sped away.

Anna stood watching until the flashing light on the back of his bike disappeared around the corner. She had a funny, floating feeling in her chest.

Finally, she turned and walked slowly to her house. She knew she was going to get it from her mom. *But it was worth it,* Anna thought. *It was definitely worth it.*

Chapter Nine

"Anna . . ."

Anna slowly opened her eyes. She could tell by the deep blackness of her room that it was very late at night. She glanced at the digital clock on her nightstand. The glowing green numbers read 1:46.

I dreamed someone was calling my name, she thought sleepily.

She was just about to snuggle under the covers, when she heard it again, louder. Impatient.

"Anna!"

Anna jerked upright. Someone *was* calling her name. It sounded like it had come from outside.

Holding her breath, she tiptoed over to the window and pushed back the curtain. In the cherry tree next to the house, she saw a dark figure crouched among the branches.

Anna sucked in her breath. She was about to scream, when the figure moved and she caught a glimpse of one long braid. "Emma?" she whispered.

"Anna! Come out and play." Emma's voice was light and crooning. Anna could see her silver eyes shining in the moonlight.

Anna undid the lock and slid open the window. Cold air rushed in against her face. "What are you doing?" she whispered. "I can't come out. It's nighttime."

"Come play with me!" Emma stood up on her branch. *"You haven't played with me in such a long time —"*

"Careful! Emma, what are you doing? You'll —" Anna gasped as Emma slipped from the tree.

But she didn't fall. She floated gently to the ground, as if she weighed no more than a feather.

How could Emma float?

"I must be dreaming," Anna said to herself. What a clear dream it was! Everything seemed so real. Her arms prickled with goose bumps. Somewhere in the neighborhood she could hear a dog barking.

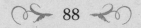 88

"Anna!" Emma called again. She was standing on the lawn now. Above her the bright, round moon looked like a coin in the sky, a shiny silver dollar. Anna was overcome with the urge to reach out and grab it. But —

"I can't get down," Anna said sadly. Oh, how she wanted to go out and play!

"Climb down." Emma pointed to the side of the house, where withering wisteria vines twined around a latticework trellis.

Anna had done this so many times in the bathroom at school she could have done it in her sleep. Hoisting herself onto the window ledge, she swung a leg over. She had to stretch to reach the trellis, but she managed to hook a foot in without too much trouble. As she climbed down, trying not to tangle her feet in the dry vines, she marveled at how real the leaves felt against her face, even though she knew she was dreaming.

Emma was back in the tree, hanging from a branch by her knees. Anna walked over to her, the cold grass numbing her bare toes.

"You came out!" Emma sang, swinging gently back and forth.

"Yes, we can play now! What should we play?"

 89

Anna felt like a little girl again. Like magic was possible, and anything could happen.

Emma's back was to Anna as she swung back and forth on the branch. Suddenly, she flipped over, her feet hitting the ground. When she straightened up, Anna stepped back with a gasp. Emma's face was twisted in a frightening sneer — and her silver eyes were *glowing.*

"You've been a naughty girl, Anna." Emma growled. *"You've been ignoring me."*

"No I haven't." Anna shivered. She was starting to not like this dream anymore.

Emma's lips peeled back from her teeth in a snarl. *"So Benny's your new best friend? Is that it? Anna and Benny sittin' in a tree. K-I-S-S-I-N-G . . ."* she taunted. *"I thought we were friends, Anna. Best friends."*

"We are friends!" Anna cried, stumbling backward.

"Not just friends. Bessssst friends." Emma came closer. In the moonlight her braids seemed to twist like snakes.

Anna clamped her hands over her eyes. "It's just a dream," she told herself. "Wake up!"

"You shouldn't have left me, Anna," Emma hissed. *"You're going to be sorry. You and Benny, you'll both be so sssssorry. . . ."*

"Wake up!" Anna yelled at herself. "Wake up! Wake up! Wake up!"

"Wake up, Anna!"

Anna opened her eyes. Her room was filled with early morning light. Someone was knocking at her door. "Mmmm," she groaned sleepily, hoping they'd go away.

"Time to get up!" Her father opened the door and came into her room. "Jeez, kiddo, it's freezing in here. What's the window doing open?"

"The window?" Anna sat up in bed. The sash was thrown all the way up. She didn't remember opening it in the night.

"*Brrr.* It must be forty degrees in here," said her dad as he shut it. "Come on, up and at 'em. You slept through your alarm. Better hustle, or you're going to be late."

As soon as he was gone, Anna leaned back on the pillows. She felt stiff and exhausted, as if she'd hardly slept at all. Bits of her dream floated back to her: the brightness of the moon, the cold, wet grass — it was all so vivid.

"Like it was real," Anna murmured.

That's stupid, she thought. Why was she getting all worked up over a dream? She laughed at herself as she climbed out of bed and headed for the shower. But she felt a lingering uneasiness.

It wasn't until she was standing under the warm spray of water that Anna started to feel better. She remembered her "date" with Benny from the day before, and her heart gave a little hop of happiness at the thought.

Anna and Benny sittin' in a tree, K-I-S-S-I-N-G . . .

An image of Emma's sneering face flashed through Anna's brain. Quickly, she shook it away. She couldn't imagine why she'd dreamed such a thing. Sure, Emma had seemed upset the day before at lunch. She'd probably just been in a bad mood, Anna reasoned. Anna would talk to her today and get it all straightened out.

But she didn't see Emma at all that morning. She didn't come by Anna's locker, and Anna didn't see her anywhere in the halls. Anna worried all through her morning classes, wondering if Emma was still mad at her.

When it was time for science class, Anna's spirits lifted. At least she'd see Benny! She hurried to class and was the first one to take her seat.

Anna watched the rest of the students file in. Dory was back at school. She walked in with her chin held high, never once looking in Anna's direction. *Fine,* Anna thought angrily, *two can play at that game.*

By the time the bell rang, Benny still hadn't showed up. Anna stared at his empty seat, crestfallen. Where was he? she wondered. Sick? He'd seemed fine the day before.

"Did you hear what happened to Benny?" said a voice behind her. It was Krystal, gossiping with her lab partner as usual.

Anna whipped around in her seat. "What about him?"

"He had a big accident last night." Krystal widened her eyes in phony alarm, clearly relishing the attention.

Anna's mouth felt dry. "What kind of accident?"

Krystal shrugged. "Nobody knows. But I heard he'll be out of school for weeks. At least, that's what his mother told the school secretary. I was in the office when she called," she added importantly.

"Girls?" Mr. Cooper said sharply from the front of the room, giving them a warning look.

Anna turned back around in her seat, trying to process this information. What Krystal said couldn't be true — could it? Krystal often got her facts wrong. But then again, she said she'd heard it from the school secretary.

Finally, Anna decided there was only one thing to do — she would go to his house and see for herself.

As soon as school was over that afternoon, she walked the few blocks to Benny's house. Her heart pounded as she rang the bell.

After a long moment, a petite dark-haired woman opened the door. "Yes?"

Anna introduced herself. "I have class with Benny," she explained. "I heard he was sick, so I, um, brought his homework." Anna had worked out that excuse in class that afternoon. "Is he, um, okay?"

"He'll be okay eventually, although I don't think he's ready for any homework yet," the woman said. She looked tired and worried. "But you can go see him, if you like. He's in his room." She moved aside and held the door open.

As Anna stepped inside, right away she noticed the hush, an unnatural quiet, as if the whole house was holding its breath. She knew then that Krystal had been right — something really bad *had* happened.

"It's the first door at the top of stairs," Benny's mother told Anna.

Anna climbed the stairs slowly, a little afraid of what she would find. When she reached the door, she took a deep breath, then gently pushed it open.

Benny was lying in bed, a blanket pulled over half his body. One leg was in a plaster cast, and a bandage was wrapped around his head. His closed eyes looked sunken in his face.

"Benny?" Anna murmured.

His eyes fluttered open. Anna smiled and started to step toward him, but the look on his face stopped her. "What are you doing here?" he said sharply.

"I brought your science homework, and, um . . ." Anna's voice faltered. Why did he keep looking at her like that . . . like he was afraid of her?

Benny was struggling to sit up. "Who let you in here?"

"Your mom," Anna said. "I heard at school that you got hurt. I just wanted to see how you were doing."

"You wanted to see how I was *doing*?" Benny blinked, as if he couldn't believe what he was hearing. "How did you think I'd be doing?"

Was this one of his weird jokes? "I don't get it, Benny," she said. "What happened to you?"

"You tell me," Benny shot back. "Why were you here last night?"

"What?" Anna stared at him.

"Don't pretend you don't know. I *saw* you."

"Saw me where? What are you talking about?"

"Last night, you were in my backyard," Benny said. "I was sleeping when I heard someone call my name. It was you, Anna."

"You must have been dreaming," Anna told him. "I wasn't here last night. I was home sleeping."

Benny shook his head, growing more agitated. "I wasn't dreaming. I saw you, Anna. And I know you saw me. You waved at me. You called my name. I leaned out the window to see what you wanted, and then . . . something pushed me."

Anna felt a shiver run down her spine. "You imagined it, Benny. I wasn't here."

"Stop *lying*, Anna. *I saw you!*" Benny's voice rose to a shout. *"Just tell me what happened!"*

Anna shook her head to say she didn't know. She

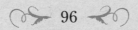

had a cold feeling in her stomach, as if she'd swallowed a gallon of ice water.

"Are you afraid I'm going to tell on you? Is that it?" he snarled. "Well, you don't have to worry. I didn't. Everyone thinks I was sleepwalking. My mom didn't find me until morning. She got up to let the cat in, and there I was, lying on the ground. She thought I was dead. And now I can't play hockey. They said it could take up to two months for my leg to heal, maybe more. They won't let me play this year if I miss two months of practice."

A tuft of hair was sticking up on the back of his head, like ruffled feathers. Anna felt an urge to reach out and smooth it down. Instead, she took a deep breath.

"Benny, I swear to you, I don't know who you saw last night, but it wasn't me. I swear it."

Benny gave her a long look, and for a moment Anna thought he believed her. But he shook his head. "You're not who I thought you were, Anna. Go away. I don't want to talk to you anymore."

Anna quietly left the room. Her legs were trembling as she made her way down the stairs to the front door. She was relieved not to run into Benny's mother on the way out.

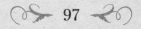

Outside, she felt tears pressing at the back of her eyes. What was going on? Why was Benny saying those terrible things about her?

He said he hit his head, Anna reminded herself. She had heard her mother tell stories about the crazy things people did and said when they had head injuries. Maybe something had happened to Benny's brain so he imagined things that he thought were real.

Yes, Anna decided. *That must be what happened. He's just confused now. When he gets better, he'll realize that none of it is true.*

But she couldn't shake the image of his eyes, glaring at her with hot hatred. His eyes had been so clear. He hadn't seemed confused at all.

Chapter Ten

The next day, Anna was more anxious than ever to talk to Emma. She had to tell someone about the strange things Benny had said. But Emma seemed to be avoiding her. Once or twice, Anna thought she saw her in the hall, but Emma always disappeared before Anna could catch up with her.

At lunchtime, Anna planted herself next to Emma's locker, determined to stay there until her friend arrived.

A few lockers down, Jessamyn and her friends were clustered in a group, talking. Jessamyn kept glancing over at Anna. She seemed to be growing more and more annoyed.

Finally, Jessamyn strode over to her. "What do you think you're doing?" she snarled at Anna, putting her face so close that Anna could smell the bubble gum on her breath.

Anna was startled, but she tried not to show it. "Nothing that's any of your business," she snapped back.

"You're always hanging around here, watching me and my friends," Jessamyn accused. "It's creepy."

Anna suddenly felt a surge of rage. "I'm not watching you, you self-absorbed twit."

Jessamyn's mouth formed a perfect lip-glossed O. But she recovered in a millisecond. "Loser," she hissed at Anna.

A few weeks ago, that very word had cut Anna to the core. But now it made her seethe with anger. "So what are you going to do? Spray paint 'Loser' on my lawn?"

"What are you talking about?" Jessamyn snapped.

"Does 'Dorky Dory' ring a bell?" Anna asked coolly. "Humiliating people in their very own homes. Is that what you and your friends do for fun these days?"

Jessamyn glared at her. "I never did that! Who told you I did that?"

Anna shook her head. "I knew you were a jerk, Jessamyn. I didn't know you were a liar, too."

Jessamyn was about to reply when a tall boy Anna had never seen before tapped her on the shoulder. "Um, could you guys move this somewhere else?"

Jessamyn spun on him. "Butt out!" she snapped.

"I would," said the boy, "but you're blocking my locker."

Surprised, Anna stepped out of the way. She watched the boy open what she'd thought was Emma's locker. *That's weird,* she thought. *How did I get that wrong?*

Jessamyn shot Anna one last poisonous look, then stalked back to her friends, her hair swishing behind her. Anna's knees were still shaking as she made her way back to her own locker, but she was smiling, too. She couldn't believe she'd stood up to Jessamyn.

It's because of Emma, Anna thought. Emma made her feel strong and brave, like she could do anything. Emma was the coolest person Anna knew, and she was . . . right there, standing in front of Anna's locker!

"Emma!" Anna rushed over to her. "I've been dying to talk to you. Something really weird happened yesterday. With Benny."

Emma smiled, almost as if she hadn't heard her. "I'm so hungry!" she said, widening her eyes in exaggeration. "Let's go out to lunch. My treat."

"Emma —"

"Don't worry. No dine and ditch. I've got money today."

Emma reached into her pocket and pulled out a wallet. It was made of pink leather, with a little ladybug charm attached to the zipper.

"Fine," Anna said with a sigh. She didn't care where they went, as long as they could talk.

When the halls were clear, they headed out a side door and walked to the deli where they'd gotten lunch on the first day they met. On the way, Anna told Emma about Benny — first about their afternoon at Moxie, then about his accident and the strange things he'd said when she went to visit him.

"I told you he was a twerp," Emma said when she was done. "He's just messing with you."

"Messing with me? How could he be *messing* with me? He really got hurt."

"So?" said Emma. "What makes you think that has anything to do with you? People get hurt all the time. Is that your fault?"

"No. But he *said* it was my fault somehow. He said he saw me. Why would he say that?"

"Oh, don't be dense, Anna," Emma snapped. "Isn't it obvious? He said it so he wouldn't have to hang out with you anymore."

Anna pulled up short and stared at her. "What?"

"Come on," Emma said, stopping too, "you didn't really think a guy like Benny would go for you."

Anna felt as if she'd been punched in the stomach. She wasn't sure which hurt more — that Emma would say such a thing, or that it might be true.

"Think back," Emma told her. "He was there with all his friends, right? They were probably laughing at you behind your back."

Anna thought about the afternoon at Moxie. She remembered how Benny's friends had smirked when he left with Anna. At the time, she'd assumed they were just teasing him. But maybe there had been another reason.

Emma slid an arm around her shoulders. "Forget about him, Anna," she murmured. "He's a jerk. They're all jerks. You and I, we're the only ones who can count on each other."

Anna felt tears pressing against the backs of her eyes, but she didn't want to cry. She clenched her jaw, telling herself, *Benny is just a jerk. He doesn't matter. He's nothing to me,* until the tears went away.

At the deli, Emma bought lunch just as she'd promised, pulling a twenty-dollar bill from her wallet with a little flourish. The day was moderately warm, so they ate again in the little park across the street. Emma kept up a cheery dialogue, but Anna couldn't enjoy her lunch. Each bite of sandwich turned to sawdust in her mouth, and she finally threw it away.

When they got back to school, they noticed a small commotion down the hall from Anna's locker. A bunch of kids were clustered around Jessamyn's locker. Lauren had her arm around Jessamyn, who seemed to be upset.

"I wonder what happened," Anna said.

"Poor little Jessamyn," Emma sneered. "Probaby broke a nail."

Anna nodded numbly. She was too unhappy to give Jessamyn much thought.

The bell rang, signaling the end of lunch period. Almost instantly, the hallway flooded with kids coming back from the cafeteria.

"Well," said Emma, turning to her. "It's been fun. See you on the flip side." She gave Anna a wink and headed off, blending into the crowded hallway.

Anna turned back to her locker and slowly collected her books. It wasn't until she was on her way to Spanish class that she thought that had been a strange thing to say. *See you on the flip side.* What did *that* mean?

Anna was still thinking about Benny in math, her last class of the day, when the office messenger came in. The messenger handed a note to the teacher, who unfolded it and scanned it quickly. "Anna?"

Her head jerked up. "Me?"

"You're wanted in Ms. Turk's office. Take your things with you."

All eyes in the classroom swiveled to Anna. Ms. Turk was the dean of the school. Students were only called to her office when they were in trouble.

Anna's heart began to pound as she stood and collected her books. She guessed someone had seen her and Emma sneaking off campus for lunch and ratted them out. She wondered how much trouble she was in.

The door to Ms. Turk's office was open, but Anna knocked anyway. The dean waved her inside and pointed wordlessly to a chair across from her desk. Anna perched on the edge of the chair.

The dean folded her hands on her desk and eyed Anna. She was a stout woman with a pointy nose and sharp, beady eyes that reminded Anna of a weasel.

"Now," said the dean, "can you tell me why I've called you in here?"

Anna weighed her options and decided to play it safe. She gave her head a tiny shake.

"Do you know a girl named Jessamyn Ito?"

"Everyone knows Jessamyn," Anna replied.

The dean picked up a pen and tapped the end of it against her desk. "Jessamyn's wallet was stolen from her locker today. Do you know anything about that?"

Anna began to relax. She hadn't been caught skipping school after all! "No," she told the dean. Then, as an afterthought, she added, "Jessamyn's friends are always hanging out by her locker. Have you talked to them?"

"Yes, I have," Ms. Turk replied. "Jessamyn's friends say that *you* are often hanging around her locker, too. You aren't friends with Jessamyn, are you?"

"No, ma'am."

"So can you tell me why you might be hanging around Jessamyn's locker when you don't have a reason to be there?"

Worry began to creep back in. *Was this some kind of setup?* Anna wondered. Was Jessamyn getting her back for their argument this morning? "My friend's locker is near Jessamyn's. I was waiting for her."

"Oh?" The dean's eyebrows arched. "What's your friend's name?"

"Emma," said Anna. "Emma Diablo."

The dean made a note on a pad on her desk. Then she set the pen down and gave Anna a long look. "Anna, we take theft in this school very seriously. We get the police involved if we have to."

She thinks I did it! Anna realized with dismay. Whatever Jessamyn had told the dean had convinced her that Anna was the thief. For a moment, Anna's rage at this injustice overcame her worry. She could feel her face turning red.

The dean's eyes narrowed. "For the last time, are you *sure* you don't know anything about Jessamyn's wallet?"

Anna pressed her lips together and shook her head. As she did, an image flashed through her mind: a little pink wallet with a ladybug charm. *Emma's wallet.*

No, Anna thought, as the truth dawned on her. *Emma wouldn't have a wallet like that. But Jessamyn would.*

Something must have showed on her face, because the dean leaned forward. "Anna? Is there something you want to tell me?"

Anna shook her head again. At that moment, all she wanted was to get out of there and find Emma. She had to ask her what was going on.

Ms. Turk sighed. "Anna, you realize I'm going to have to search your locker."

"What? Now?" Anna blurted. She didn't have time for this. She had to find Emma!

"Yes, now," the dean said sternly. "Come with me, young lady."

As the dean marched her down the hall, Anna felt as if her feet were moving in slow motion. But her mind was churning.

It can't be true. Emma wouldn't have stolen anything, she told herself. *She breaks the rules sometimes, but she would never actually* steal.

But she did *steal,* said another voice in Anna's mind. *She stole those cans of paint from the art* room. *And dining and ditching — that was steal-ing, too.*

Come to think of it, Anna had never seen Emma pay for anything. Even when she brought chips and candy for lunch, she pulled them out of her pockets, not from a bag like anyone else would have.

Anna suddenly felt certain that Emma was in big trouble. Was there some way she could warn her? Frantically, she tried to remember what class Emma was in — Spanish, PE? She realized she didn't know Emma's schedule at all.

They had arrived at Anna's locker. "Go ahead," Ms. Turk ordered. "Open it."

Anna slowly spun the combination. *The bell is going to ring soon,* she told herself. *Then school will be out for the day. I'll find Emma right after school.*

These were the thoughts that were going through Anna's mind as she swung open her locker door. At once, she forgot everything she'd been thinking.

There, on the top shelf of her locker, was the pink wallet with the ladybug charm. Anna noticed a detail that she'd missed when the wallet had been in Emma's hand — a name stitched across the flap in white thread: *Jessamyn.*

Chapter Eleven

Anna stared at the wallet, hardly able to believe her eyes. "I — I didn't take it!" she stuttered. "She must have put it there."

Ms. Turk's face was grim. "I very much doubt that Jessamyn broke into your locker to leave *her* wallet there."

Anna hadn't meant Jessamyn, of course. *But why would Emma do it?* she wondered. Emma was her friend.

"You're in very big trouble, young lady." Ms. Turk grabbed the wallet with one hand and Anna with the other. Her grip was surprisingly strong. It felt like a steel clamp on Anna's shoulder.

As the dean dragged Anna back to her office, the final bell jangled overhead. All up and down the hall, classroom doors popped open, and students spilled out into the hall. When they saw the dean and Anna coming, they got out of the way, like the sea parting. Anna was aware of kids staring at her as she passed. At one point she caught a glimpse of Dory, her eyes goggling at Anna from behind her thick glasses.

"It's a mistake, Ms. Turk," Anna kept pleading. "If you'll just let me explain. . . ."

"You can do your explaining when your parents get here," the dean replied as they entered her office.

My parents? Anna's heart sank. "Please don't call them," she begged. "I'll tell you everything."

So, feeling like a traitor, she told the dean about Emma, how she'd offered to buy Anna lunch at the deli and paid for it with money from the pink wallet.

The dean's frown deepened. "The deli? You mean, you *left* school? You know you aren't allowed to leave the school grounds during school hours."

Oops. Now she'd really done it. She was only digging them both in deeper.

"Yes, ma'am," Anna said miserably.

"Is this the first time you've done this?"

"Yes," Anna lied.

"All right, go ahead." The dean nodded.

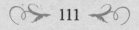

"That's it. Emma paid for lunch and we ate it and we came back. That's all, I swear. I didn't know she stole the wallet," she added. Anna was afraid to say more until she found out what was going on.

"And how did the wallet end up in your locker?" asked the dean.

Anna shook her head. "I don't know, ma'am." That was the part that baffled her, too. She believed Emma had put it there — but why?

"Anna, since the wallet was found in your locker, you are clearly involved. I'm going to have to call your parents. You may wait outside my office."

There was a small vestibule outside the dean's office, which was empty except for two hard plastic chairs. Anna plopped down in one, a puddle of misery. As the minutes ticked by, she kept thinking of Emma and the wallet, going over and over things in her mind. Why had she left it there? *When* had she left it there?

"Anna, what is going on?!" Anna's mother stood in the doorway. The collar of her coat was rolled under on one side, and her hair was sticking out in every direction. She had clearly come as quickly as she could.

As soon as Anna saw her, the tears that had

been lurking behind her eyes spilled over. "I didn't do it, Mom!"

"Didn't do what? Tell me what happened." Mrs. Dipalo sat down in the other chair and listened as Anna briefly explained what had happened. She felt like she was betraying Emma. But what choice did she have?

To Anna's astonishment, her mother didn't seem angry, only concerned. "We'll get this straightened out, sweetie," she said, patting Anna's knee. "The dean will talk to Emma and her parents, and everything will get straightened out."

Even if we do, Anna thought, *Emma will never be my friend again.*

For a while they sat in silence, waiting for the dean. Anna leaned forward, with her elbows on her knees, staring at an old stain on the dingy gray carpet. Her mother sat with her head tipped back, staring into space.

"Emma," she murmured. Her eyes were distant, as if she was remembering something. "The girl with silver eyes."

Anna's head snapped up. "What did you say?"

Her mother glanced over at her. "Oh, nothing. I was just remembering something you used to say when you were little, about your imaginary friend, Emma. Once I asked you what she looked like, and you told me, 'Mommy, she has silver eyes.' I always remembered that, because I thought it was so funny." Mrs. Dipalo shook her head. "I don't know why I'm thinking about this now."

At that moment, the door to the dean's office opened. Anna's mother stood up quickly. "Hello," she said. "I'm Anna's mother," she said.

"Mrs. Dipalo, thank you for coming," the dean replied. "As you've heard, Anna has run into some trouble."

"Anna was just telling me about it," said her mother. "And what about the other girl, Emma? Were you able to get in touch with her parents?"

The dean was silent for a moment. "Mrs. Dipalo, have you ever met Emma?"

"No, I haven't yet. But Anna has told me a little about her. Why?"

The dean's eyes flicked to Anna. "I've just been checking our records. There is no Emma Diablo. We've never had a student by that name."

Chapter Twelve

"That's not true!" Anna blurted out, stunned. What was going on? Was this some kind of trick? "I know Emma goes to school here," she told the dean. "I see her here every day."

The dean folded her arms across her chest, her nostrils pinching as she drew in a long breath. "Anna," she said in a flinty voice, "I think it's time you start telling the truth."

"I *am* telling the truth. Emma took the wallet. She's the one you need to talk to." Anna turned to her mother. "Mom, you believe me, right?"

Her mother looked back and forth between Anna and the dean, clearly confused. "Perhaps there's been some kind of mistake?" she ventured hesitantly.

"Could Emma possibly go by another name in her records?"

"I've checked our entire database," Ms. Turk replied. "We have no students with the last name Diablo."

"Well, maybe I got her last name wrong," Anna said, though she knew she hadn't. She clearly remembered Emma's words on the day they'd met. *Diablo, 'cause I'm devilish.* Had Emma lied about her name?

"Do you know anything else about Emma?" her mother prompted. "Her parents' names? Where she lives?"

Anna shook her head, realizing how foolish she appeared. How could she not know where her best friend lived? And why hadn't it ever occurred to her to ask?

"Her phone number?" Ms. Turk added in a tone that made it clear she didn't expect much from Anna.

But Anna brightened. "I know her cell number. And her locker is on the first floor west hallway. Number two thirty-five. Or — or maybe it's two thirty-six," she added, remembering her confusion that morning.

Ms. Turk picked up her phone and pressed the line to the school secretary. "Ellen," she said, "will you please look up the students assigned to these locker numbers?" She gave the numbers Anna had mentioned.

As she set the phone down, Anna felt a pang of guilt. She didn't want to get her friend in trouble — but she didn't want to take the blame for something she hadn't done, either. She hoped Emma would understand.

But she never had the chance to find out. Neither of the numbers Anna gave the dean checked out. Lockers 235 and 236 were assigned to two eighth grade boys. Emma's cell phone number led only to a message saying the number was not in service.

Anna listened to each call with a growing sense of helplessness. She didn't understand what was going on. But whatever it was, she was starting to realize she was in it alone.

Ms. Turk hung up the phone and leaned back in her chair. "Now," she said, gazing sternly at Anna, "are you going to tell us the truth?"

The next hour went by in a blur. No matter how much Anna swore she was innocent, the dean refused to believe her. The School Resource Officer was called in, and they decided Anna would be given a week of in-school suspension. Throughout the discussion, Anna's mother kept nodding and saying things like, "Yes, we understand," and "Of course, Ms. Turk," and at some point Anna realized her mom was no longer on her side. She wouldn't even look at Anna.

After that they made Anna step out of the office, while the dean and her mother spoke to the school counselor. Anna could only guess what they were saying about her.

By the time they left the school, she felt exhausted. The rain had finally let up, but dark clouds still blanketed the sky, and the air had turned colder. As they hurried toward her mother's car, a raw, icy wind whipped Anna's face, as if even the weather had turned against her.

"Mom," Anna tried one last time once they were driving, "I know Ms. Turk doesn't believe me, but I swear I didn't steal anything. It was Emma —"

"Oh, Anna." Her mother turned to her with such a look of dismay that Anna's mouth snapped shut. They rode the rest of the way home in silence.

At home, Anna climbed the stairs to her room and lay down on her bed. She stared up at the ceiling. Her father would be home soon, and she dreaded having to tell him what had happened that day. He would be crushed to find out that his daughter was a thief.

But I'm not *a thief,* Anna reminded herself. She went through the day's events for what seemed like the hundredth time: Emma's mysterious comment, the strange appearance of Jessamyn's wallet in her locker, the phone and locker numbers that didn't check out . . .

Where is Emma? Anna wondered. Why didn't they have a record of her at school? And, more importantly, had Emma known what was going to happen? Was she trying to set Anna up? But *why?*

Somewhere behind the questions crowding her brain there was a steady rhythm at the back of her mind. Anna suddenly realized that she was repeating a number over and over again to herself. *Nine-four-nine-oh-six-one-five.* It was Emma's phone number. An unusual number, Anna thought. Most numbers in their area started with five. And yet to Anna it was oddly familiar.

Abruptly, she sat up and got a piece of paper from her desk. It wasn't until she wrote the number down that she realized why it was familiar: it was her own phone number, backward.

Anna felt a cold pit at the bottom of her stomach. She knew it couldn't be coincidence. But Emma had given Anna her number first — not the other way around. How could Emma have known Anna's number before they'd even met?

Something else was bothering Anna. *Emma, the girl with the silver eyes,* her mother had said. *Your imaginary friend.*

Anna was certain she'd never described Emma to her parents. Could her mother have seen Emma somewhere? But then why bring up her imaginary friend?

A horrible possibility was starting to form in Anna's mind. Was Emma . . . could she be . . . *imaginary?*

"No! That's insane," Anna said aloud. If Emma was imaginary, that meant she didn't really exist. And Emma most certainly existed. Anna thought of all the things they'd done together — climbing up to the school roof, throwing ketchup bombs on the Jackals, skipping school, eating lunch at the diner.

Anna would never have done those things alone; they wouldn't have even occurred to her.

Besides, she knew Emma was real. Anna had grasped her hand. She had braided her hair. And, if Anna needed any more proof, it was right there on her pinky finger.

Anna stared at the friendship ring Emma had given her. *But you've always had that ring,* said a little voice in her head. *Remember? You've had it since you were a little girl.*

Anna ran her hands through her hair. *I can't believe I'm even thinking this,* she told herself. *Emma is just a regular girl who goes to Wilson. That idiot dean might not know her, but plenty of other people do. Like the kids in her classes, like . . . like . . .*

Try as she might, Anna couldn't come up with a single name. She realized she'd never seen Emma talking to anyone else at school. Every time Anna had encountered her — in the hallway, in the bathroom, on the roof — she had always been alone, always waiting for Anna.

As if, Anna thought with growing alarm, *she existed for me.*

"This is crazy. This is crazy. This is crazy." Anna leaped up from her bed and began to pace around her room. Her eyes fell on the cork bulletin board next to her desk. It was covered with photos of her and Dory. Anna was so used to the pictures that even after they'd stopped being friends, she'd never thought to take them down. Now she found herself staring at years and years of snapshots: Anna and Dory as little girls, having a tea party in Anna's backyard; the two of them in party hats, blowing out the candles on Anna's birthday cake; as kindergarteners, dressed as black cats for Halloween; in sixth grade, wearing sunglasses and mugging for the camera . . .

All I need is a photo of Emma to prove that she's real, Anna thought. But she didn't have one. Why didn't she have one? Normal friends had pictures of each other!

At the bottom of the corkboard, Anna had tacked up an old drawing of her and Dory. Two stick figures with a rainbow arching over their heads. Anna had drawn the picture in first grade. In one corner of the page, in clumsy, childish handwriting, she had written *beSt frenDS*.

Staring at the old picture gave Anna an idea. It was an absurd, ridiculous idea. *But,* Anna thought in desperation, *I have to know.*

She opened the door to her bedroom and crept downstairs. The house seemed cold and dark. For the first time in Anna's memory, there were no comforting dinnertime smells coming from the kitchen. This was one day that wouldn't be fixed by a hot meal.

Anna heard voices in the living room and realized her father was home. She'd been so wrapped up in her thoughts she hadn't heard him come in. She tiptoed closer and paused just outside the living room, listening.

"The school counselor believes she may have a conduct disorder," her mother was saying.

"What does that mean, exactly? A conduct disorder?" Anna's father asked.

"It's considered an early sign of criminal behavior." Her mother's voice was strained. "The counselor said that if she continues with these sorts of problems, it's likely she'll be expelled. She could end up in juvenile detention." Mrs. Dipalo was silent for a moment. "The counselor said children with conduct disorders can grow up to be sociopaths." On the last word her voice cracked. Anna could tell that she was crying.

A sociopath? Like a crazy person? Anna didn't want to hear any more. She moved past the living room, down the hall to the small room that served as both an office and an extra bedroom. It contained a desk, a daybed, and an old bureau.

The bottom drawer of the bureau contained a treasure trove of Anna's old things: finger paintings, ribbons from school fairs, reports with gold stars pasted at the top. Anna dug through messy collages encrusted with glitter and dried macaroni, pictures made from pipe cleaners, and a handmade card with the message *Hapy Muthers day. I luv you mom!*

She dug deeper. At last, on an old piece of printer paper shoved near the back of the drawer, she found what she was looking for. It was a clumsy crayon drawing of two girls holding hands. They had blobs for heads, sticks for bodies, and arms and hands like lollipops. The girl on the left had two brown dots for eyes and a big red smile.

But it was the girl on the right that held Anna's attention. Her eyes were colored in silver crayon.

Anna turned the page over. Any doubt she might have had vanished when she saw the note on the back in her mother's tidy handwriting:

A-NNA, AGE 4
"ME AND EMMA"

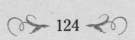

Anna stared at the words until they started to blur. She set the drawing down and closed her eyes, trying to make sense of the thoughts that were swirling through her head.

Could she really have imagined her entire friendship with Emma? Anna tried to think of any other possible explanation — any reason that her new friend Emma might resemble her old made-up friend — but she came up with nothing. She didn't have a single shred of hard evidence that Emma really existed.

Except one thing, Anna told herself. *Jessamyn's wallet. How else did it get in my locker?*

An icy shudder went down Anna's spine as the truth slowly dawned on her. If Emma wasn't real, there could only be one explanation: that Emma and Anna were the same person. Anna had stolen the wallet herself, without even realizing what she was doing. It meant she really was crazy.

Chapter Thirteen

Anna had a hard time falling asleep that night. When she finally did she had terrible dreams: she was caught in a giant spiderweb, fighting to get free, but the more she struggled the more entangled she became. And when the spider appeared, it had her own face. . . .

She awoke in a tangle of bedsheets, exhausted and shaken. Anna climbed out of bed and went over to the mirror above her dresser. Her hair was a dark snarl around her pale face, and there were shadows like bruises under her eyes.

"Are you crazy?" she asked herself. Her reflection gave no reply.

Breakfast that morning was a silent meal. The night before, her parents had decided her punishment:

she was grounded for a month, and they expected her to come home right after school every day — no exceptions. Her father was even going to start leaving work early to be home with her. But now, having delivered her sentence, they seemed to have nothing left to say to Anna. All that morning they kept sneaking looks at her as if they were no longer sure who she was.

Anna wasn't so sure herself.

She was almost relieved when it was time to go to school. But once she got there, she wished she was home again. She felt on edge, expecting to see Emma at any moment.

And then what? she wondered. *How does it work when you're crazy?* Anna decided that if she saw Emma, she wouldn't speak to her. The least she could do was *act* sane.

She was so wrapped up in these thoughts that it was a moment before she noticed something weird going on. In the hallways, kids were turning to stare at her. A few girls moved their handbags to their other shoulders as she passed.

It wasn't until she got to her locker that Anna understood. The word *THIEF* was scrawled across her locker in heavy black marker.

As she gaped at the word, she felt someone yank one of her braids. Hard.

"Ouch!" Anna whirled around and came face-to-face with Kima.

"You are so dead," Kima murmured, her eyes glittering dangerously. Then she sauntered off down the hall.

The next week was the worst of Anna's life. She spent every hour of her in-school suspension shut up in a tiny room next to Ms. Turk's office. She was allowed to leave only to use the bathroom and to get lunch from the cafeteria. But these moments were hardly a relief. The other students treated her like an outcast, and she lived in fear of running into Jessamyn and her friends. Anna had never felt so alone.

The strange thing was, she never saw Emma. *Where was she?* The question began to obsess Anna. After so many hours alone in the detention room, she was almost starting to miss her friend, imaginary or not.

On the Friday after Anna returned to her regular classes, she was sitting in English when a note arrived from the office.

"Anna?" said her teacher. "You're wanted in Ms. Turk's office."

Again? What now? Anna wondered as she collected her books.

She arrived at the office to find the dean red in the face. "Come with me," Ms. Turk ordered, marching her down the hall toward the gymnasium.

They stopped in front of the old girls' bathroom.

Someone had written in red spray paint on the door of the bathroom:

EMMA LIVES!

"What is the meaning of this?" the dean demanded.

Anna felt her blood run cold, but she tried to keep her face composed. "What makes you think I'd know?"

"Emma? Wasn't that the name of your 'friend'?" the dean replied, frowning.

Anna stared at the graffiti. The red paint had dripped down the door, giving the words a sinister look. "Anybody could have written it," she said. But she didn't think that just "anybody" had.

"There are two other Emmas at this school, and I have spoken to them both. Neither one knows anything about this," the dean added.

"Well, I don't know anything about it, either. I've been in class all morning," Anna told Ms. Turk. "You can ask my teachers."

"I certainly will." The dean's eyes bore into Anna. Though it took every fiber in her being not to squirm, Anna held her gaze.

"All right," the dean said finally, "you can go back to class."

Anna hurried away, feeling both elated and frightened. Whoever she was, Emma was back. And maybe now Anna could start getting some answers.

She took her seat in science class and gazed straight ahead at the chalkboard, but her mind was racing.

She remembered the day they'd written their names on the wall of the abandoned building. That had been the day they'd promised to be friends forever. Was there some proof there? Some clue to Emma's existence?

There was one way to find out.

I can't do it, Anna told herself. Sneaking out of school was too risky. If she got caught, she'd be suspended for sure. And she was expected at home right after school.

Then she thought, *But I have to know.*

Anna waited until lunchtime, then she snuck off campus. She jogged all the way to the abandoned building. It looked the same as the first time she'd been there — empty, crumbling, forlorn. The only difference was that there seemed to be even more trash littering the lot than before.

She slipped through the broken chain-link fence and made her way around to the river side of the building.

There it was, written in bold red and black letters:

ANNA + EMMA = BEST FRIENDS FOREVER!

Feet crunched over broken glass nearby. Someone was coming! Anna spun around, expecting to see a stranger, possibly someone dangerous. All her muscles tensed to run.

"I thought I'd find you here." Emma smiled as she stepped around the side of the building. "Don't look at me like that, Anna. If I didn't know better, I'd think you weren't glad to see me."

"Who *are* you?" Anna whispered.

"Come on, you know who I am," Emma replied. "I'm your best friend. You've known me almost your whole life."

"No." Anna shook her head. "It's not possible."

"It *is* possible," Emma said, taking a step closer. "I'm here, aren't I?"

There was a look in Emma's eyes that Anna had never seen before. A greedy, hungry look that frightened Anna, and she backed away.

"You're here now, but where have you been?" she asked in a shaky voice. "You left me at school. You let me take all the blame for everything. . . ."

"Yes, I'm sorry about that. But it had to be done," Emma said matter-of-factly. "You needed to be reminded what friendship is all about."

"That's not friendship!" Anna exclaimed.

"Isn't it?" Emma's eyebrows arched. "I took the blame for you for years, Anna. Don't you remember? You blamed me for everything, and I never complained because I was your best friend. And then one day, Dory came along, and you just threw me away."

"B-but you didn't exist," Anna stuttered. "You *don't* exist —"

"Don't say that!" Emma screeched. Suddenly, she snatched up an empty glass bottle from the ground and hurled it in Anna's direction. Anna threw up her hands for protection, but the bottle smashed down next to her, spraying glass across her shoes.

"Do you need any more proof that I exist?" Emma shouted.

Anna shook her head. She was trembling all over.

At once, the anger vanished from Emma's face. "I didn't mean to scare you," she said calmly. "But you must never say that again. You must never, ever say I don't exist."

A breeze blew off the river, bringing with it the scent of mud and decay. Anna wrapped her arms around her shaking body. "What do you want from me?" she asked in a voice barely above a whisper.

"What I've always wanted, silly," Emma said. "Just your undying friendship. And now we don't have to worry about Dory or Benny or anyone else getting in the way. They don't care about you now. Nobody cares about you, do they, Anna? Nobody except me. I care."

As she spoke, Emma came closer and closer. Anna wanted to run, but her feet felt frozen to the ground. Like a mouse transfixed by a python, she found herself staring into Emma's strange silver eyes.

"Don't you see, Anna?"

On the word *see*, Emma's eyes suddenly became two silver mirrors in which Anna saw herself reflected — not the frightened girl she was now, but a powerful, strong, confident Anna.

And there was Emma by her side. For Anna saw Emma in the mirrors, too, like her own twin. And look! They were laughing — laughing at everyone else, the whole world. They were having so much fun. . . .

"Don't you remember how it used to be?" Emma said, her voice low and soothing. "It can be like that again. I've been waiting for you, Anna. Now that I'm back we'll always be friends. Best friends . . . *forever.*"

"No!"

It took every ounce of Anna's will to wrench her eyes away from that hypnotic gaze. Emma reached out as if to stop her, but Anna slithered through her grasp. Skidding across the glass-covered pavement, she darted through the fence and ran away from there as fast as she could.

Chapter Fourteen

Anna ran until she felt her lungs would burst. Her heart seemed to pound a frantic chant: *It's not possible . . . not possible . . . not possible. . . .*

She didn't stop running until she reached the school. Inside the doors she stopped, gasping for breath. She was clammy with sweat, and she shivered as she leaned against a row of lockers, trying to make sense of what had just happened.

Emma and her imaginary childhood friend were one and the same. That much was clear. By any definition of *imaginary*, that meant Emma shouldn't exist.

And yet she did exist. Somehow, Emma had become real, someone with her own mind, capable of her own actions. Actions that had real consequences.

The rational part of Anna's brain still didn't want to believe it. But in her heart she knew it was true. The reason Emma had seemed so familiar to her right from the very first time they'd met was because Anna already knew her. She had always known her.

But something still didn't make sense. If Emma truly existed, why could no one else see her?

The final lunch bell rang. The hallway started to fill with the noise of kids returning from the cafeteria. Anna watched them, feeling as if she was separated from them by an invisible pane of glass. They all seemed so happy, so normal, like they didn't have a single care. Right then, Anna would have given anything to be like them.

Anna made her way through the crowded hall, so caught up in her thoughts that she didn't notice the person in front of her until she bumped right into him.

"Hey, watch it," said a not unfriendly voice. Anna looked up and saw she'd run into Benny's friend Eamonn.

"Oh, hey." Eamonn blinked at her and shook his head. "Wow. Déjà vu."

"What?" Anna asked distractedly, barely hearing him. She was still thinking about Emma.

"I just had déjà vu," Eamonn told her. "I swear I walked past you in the West Hall less than a minute ago." He shrugged and laughed. "I must be seeing things."

Anna stared at him. The round face, the dark braids — Emma looked just like her. *That's how Emma manages to be invisible,* she realized. *Everyone thinks she's me!*

"Anna, are you okay?" Eamonn asked, frowning.

Anna didn't answer. She brushed past him and hurried down the hall, a feeling of panic rising in her. What other things had Emma done, pretending to be her?

"Benny," she whispered to herself. If what Anna suspected was true, maybe he had been telling the truth after all. Maybe he really *had* seen her the night of his accident. Or he thought he had.

And Dory, too, Anna thought. She wasn't lying when she'd blamed Anna for spray painting her lawn. She really thought she'd seen Anna outside her house that night. But why would Emma want to hurt her friends?

Almost as soon as Anna had formed the question, she knew the answer. "Because she wants me to herself," she murmured.

A bell jangled overhead, making Anna jump. She realized she was standing alone in an empty hall-way. Everyone had gone to class.

I have to talk to Dory, Anna decided. First things first — she needed to win back her old friend.

Just then, Anna saw Ms. Turk coming toward her down the hall. Anna glanced left and right, looking for an escape. But it was too late. The dean had spotted her.

"Anna Dipalo!" Ms. Turk bore down on her, look-ing like a cat that had cornered a mouse. "Why aren't you in class?"

"I was just, um, j-just going now," Anna stuttered. Ms. Turk's eyes narrowed suspiciously, and Anna realized how guilty she sounded.

"You do realize that you are on probation, young lady. Do you not?"

Anna nodded meekly.

The dean looked around the hallway, as if won-dering which locker Anna had just been pillaging. "Should I find out that anything here has gone *amiss*" — Ms. Turk drew out the word with obvious relish — "I'll have grounds for suspending you. Now get to class at once."

Anna scurried down the hall with a feeling of

dread. Ms. Turk could send her to class, but it wouldn't matter. Emma was still out there some-where. And who knew what she would do next?

The next forty minutes were agony for Anna. As her Spanish teacher dragged the class through a series of verb conjugations, Anna never took her eyes from the clock on the wall. Between each tick of the minute hand, an eternity seemed to pass.

The more Anna thought about it, the more she was sure that she had to talk to Dory. Dory was smart; she would be able to help.

When at last class was over, Anna was out of her seat before the bell had even finished ringing. She was almost to the door when her Spanish teacher, Mrs. Marcos, called out, "Anna, I'd like to see you after class."

Anna wanted to scream in frustration. But she scuffled reluctantly over to the teacher's desk.

"Anna, are you aware that you're failing this class?" the Spanish teacher asked.

Anna stared at her, confused. Failing? "I can't be," she replied. "I have an A —"

"You *had* an A," Mrs. Marcos corrected. She ran her finger down a column in her grade book. "You

haven't turned in a homework assignment in over two weeks."

Two weeks? That didn't seem right. She'd done some Spanish homework recently, hadn't she? Anna tried to think when, but she couldn't remember. There'd been so much else going on. . . .

The teacher was saying something else, and Anna abruptly tuned in. "What?"

Mrs. Marcos sighed. "I *said*, when a student starts failing, I'm required to inform her parents."

"No!" Anna blurted. "I — I mean, you don't need to tell my parents." Her parents *couldn't* find out that she was flunking, not after everything else. They'd never be able to look at her again. "Please, Mrs. Marcos. I'll start doing better. I promise."

Anna felt as if her whole life was spinning out of control. But this time Anna couldn't blame Emma, not completely. She'd done this to herself.

Mrs. Marcos pressed her lips together and gave Anna a thoughtful look. "I'll give you one week. If you can turn around your performance in class, I won't have to notify your parents."

"I will," Anna promised as she hurried toward the door. But she was thinking, *One week?* It didn't seem like much time.

She'd missed the chance to catch Dory between classes, so it was another forty minutes before she finally made her way to Dory's locker. Anna was worried that she might miss her again, so when she rounded the corner and saw her old friend standing there, she cried out with relief. "Dory!"

Dory looked over, startled, and that's when Anna realized she wasn't alone. Two girls named Melody and Kate were standing at her locker.

Anna felt a pang of despair. She'd counted on talking to Dory alone.

Still, she made her way over to them. Dory warily watched her approach.

"Hey." Anna smiled brightly, despite her anxiousness. "I was wondering if I could talk to you, Dory." She glanced at the other girls and added, "Alone?"

The way the girls' eyes snapped to Dory, Anna knew that she'd told them why they weren't friends anymore.

"All right," Dory said after a moment's pause. She turned to her friends. "I'll catch up with you guys in a minute."

Swinging their backpacks onto their shoulders, the two other girls started toward the exit doors, casting curious glances back at Anna and Dory.

Feelings of hurt and jealousy welled up in Anna. How could Dory have replaced her so quickly? "So, you've been hanging out with those girls?" she asked casually, trying not to show how stung she felt.

"Yeah," said Dory. "They're nice. We're getting ready for the dance together tonight."

"The dance?"

"The Halloween dance." Dory gave her a funny look. "Don't tell me you forgot about it."

Anna *had* forgotten about it. It seemed strange to her that other kids were still doing normal things, like going to dances. Once again she had the feeling that she was separated from everyone around her by some invisible wall.

Dory shifted her backpack uncomfortably. "So, what did you want to talk to me about?"

Anna took a deep breath. "I wanted to tell you that I'm sorry for how I've acted lately."

Dory's expression softened a little. Encouraged, Anna went on. "I know I've been kind of a jerk, but some really weird stuff has been happening. Things that are . . . hard to explain." She looked her friend in the eye, "Dory, listen, I didn't write that thing on your lawn."

At once, Dory's face closed off. "Forget it. I don't really want to hear it," she said. She slammed her locker and turned to leave.

"Dory, wait!" Anna grabbed her wrist to stop her. "You have to believe me. I wouldn't do something like that. Not to you or anyone else."

"Don't *lie*, Anna!" Dory said, twisting her arm out of Anna's grip. "I *saw* you."

"You saw someone who looked like me, but it wasn't me," Anna told her.

"Oh, so that's your story now? You're totally innocent, and it was actually your evil twin?" Dory's voice crackled with sarcasm.

This was going all wrong! Anna could feel her chance slipping away. "Dory, do you remember Emma?"

"Your new best friend?" Dory said, putting her hands on her hips and arching one eyebrow. "I can't say I ever met her. So, where is she now?"

"I meant, when we were little," Anna tried one last time. "I had an imaginary friend I called Emma?"

Anna thought she saw a flicker in Dory's eyes. Was it surprise? Fear?

"Dory, she's back," Anna whispered. "Emma's back. And this time, somehow, she's real."

Dory stared at her, and there was no mistaking the look in her eyes now. It was frank alarm. "You're crazy."

"It *sounds* crazy," Anna agreed desperately. "I know it does. But it's true. She hurt you — and other people, too. Dory, I need your help. . . ."

But Dory was backing away from her. "My friends are waiting for me. I have to go." Before Anna could stop her, she turned on her heel and hurried out the door.

Anna closed her eyes and put her face in her hands. She felt like crying, but she was too exhausted for the tears to come. She'd been so foolish. She'd thought Dory could help. But no one could help her. She was in this alone.

"Have a nice chat?" said a voice close by.

Anna's eyes flew open. Emma was standing in front of her, wearing a sneering smile.

"I don't understand it," she said to Anna. "I'm everything you've ever wanted in a friend. I'm cool. Daring. Exciting. But you *still* keep running back to Dory."

Anna shrank back against the wall, glancing around for someone . . . anyone.

"No one is going to help you, Anna," Emma said, as if she could read her mind. "No one cares about you — except me. Don't you get it? I'm your only friend now."

"Friend?" Anna burst out. "You're not my friend. You're ruining my life!"

"*What* life?" Emma sneered. "You had no life before I came along."

Anna knew Emma was right. She *was* what Anna had wanted — almost as if Anna had wished her into existence.

Emma's eyes flashed. "We'll have so much fun together," she promised. Once again, her voice was crooning, hypnotic. "We're just alike, you and me. We're two sides of the same coin. We can have so much fun together. Just promise me you'll always be my friend —"

"Stop!" Anna shouted, squeezing her eyes shut. With effort, she wrenched herself away from Emma's magnetic pull. "I'm not like you, and you're not my friend!"

"You're wrong, Anna." Emma's voice hardened.

"I'm your best friend. I should have finished this a long time ago. But you'll see. Soon, I'll be the only friend you've ever known."

"Never!" Anna cried. Her voice echoed in the empty hallway.

Anna opened her eyes and saw that she was alone. Emma was gone.

Chapter Fifteen

At home that evening, Anna paced in her bedroom. Her room was so small she could only take a few steps before she had to turn around again. Back and forth, back and forth she went, like a caged animal. She was too upset to sit still.

Soon, I'll be the only friend you've ever known. What did Emma mean? Her words echoed in Anna's head, filling her with a terrible sense of foreboding.

Downstairs, Anna heard the clatter of a pot lid in the kitchen. Her mother was cooking spaghetti again. The smell of it drifted up the stairs, but for once it wasn't comforting. Tonight, the warm, cozy house felt like a prison. Emma was out there somewhere, doing who knew what, and Anna was trapped inside, powerless to stop her.

Anna paused in front of her bedroom window, gazing out at the oncoming night. With the change of weather, the tree outside had shed most of its leaves, and now its skeletal branches reached up toward the darkening sky. For a split second Anna thought she saw a face among the branches.

Her heart skipped a beat. She leaned closer, pressing her face right up to the glass. There was no one there. The face she thought she'd seen had only been her own reflection in the windowpane. Still, Anna shivered. In that brief instant, she'd been certain she'd seen Emma.

Anna turned away and resumed her pacing, but she felt rattled. She couldn't shake the feeling that Emma was close by, watching her, shadowing her every move. . . .

"Shadowing," Anna murmured.

Her eyes fell on a photo in the collage on her corkboard. It was the picture of her and Dory on Halloween when they were four or five years old. They were dressed identically in black leotards, with whiskers painted on their faces and furry cat ears on their heads. The picture had been taken in Anna's room. Anna had her arm around her friend, grinning. Next to her, little Dory stared somberly into the camera, her forehead creased with worry.

Anna had always liked the picture. "What were you so worried about?" she'd once teased Dory. "Afraid I would get more candy than you?" But now, looking at the photo, she saw something different.

Anna pulled the photo off the corkboard and looked closer. On the wall behind Anna, there seemed to be a double shadow. Was it just a trick of the flash? Some blur of the film?

That was the night we didn't go trick-or-treating, Anna remembered. *The night Dory fell.*

A dim memory flickered in Anna's mind, like a match flaring in darkness. She and Dory were standing at the top of the stairs, just outside her room. Dory had been upset about something.

What was it? Anna squeezed her eyes shut, trying to plunge deeper into the memory. She remembered taking Dory's hand. *Don't worry,* she'd said to Dory. *I told her she can't come with us. I don't like her any more. You're my best friend now.*

The next thing she remembered was Dory tumbling head over heels down the stairs. She'd broken her arm and her collarbone. Anna's parents thought she'd slipped on the stairs.

But what if she didn't slip?

Anna's eyes opened wide as it dawned on her: *Emma pushed Dory!* That's what Emma had meant when she'd said she should have finished this a long time ago. She'd tried to hurt her once before — and now she was going to do it again.

"I have to warn Dory!" Anna said aloud. Even if Dory thought she was crazy, she had to find a way to make her friend understand that her life might be in danger!

She jumped as the door to her bedroom opened. Her father walked in. "Anna? Honey? Who are you talking to?" he asked.

"Nobody . . . nothing . . . I was just thinking aloud." Anna tried to smile.

Her father studied her with concern. "Mom asked me to let you know that dinner's ready."

"I'm not hungry." It was true. At that moment, the thought of being stuck at the dinner table turned her stomach. "I — I think I'm coming down with the flu or something. I just want to rest."

Her father started to say something, then seemed to change his mind. "Well, it'll be in the kitchen when you feel hungry." He left, shutting the door behind him.

Anna waited until she was sure her father was downstairs. Then she cracked open the door and tiptoed into the hall. When they'd grounded her, her parents had also taken away her cell phone. But there was a landline in her parents' bedroom.

Anna went into their bedroom, leaving the door slightly ajar so she could hear if one of them came up the stairs. She took the phone off its cradle on her mother's nightstand and quickly dialed Dory's cell number.

"Pick up! Pick up!" she whispered. But the phone went to voice mail.

She tried Dory's house next. On the third ring, someone picked up. "Hello?"

"Dory!" Anna exclaimed.

"No, this is Dory's mother. Who's this?" came the reply.

Dang! Anna hadn't counted on Dory's parents answering. She was sure they wouldn't be happy to hear from her after what she'd supposedly done to their lawn. But she sucked up her courage. "Hi, Mrs. Welch. It's Anna. May I please speak to Dory?"

"Dory isn't here," her mother replied in a frosty voice. "She's gone to the dance with her friends."

Anna tried to keep her voice calm. "If you hear from her, would you ask her to call me? Please tell her it's urgent." She hung up before Mrs. Welch could say no.

She had to get to the dance. But how? She was grounded — not to mention barred from all school activities. If Ms. Turk spotted her there, she'd be in trouble for sure.

If only I could be invisible, Anna thought. And then she thought of a way she could be.

Anna hurried back to her room and threw open the closet. At the back she found a shoe box full of old face paint from the year she and Dory had dressed up as scarecrows. Most of it was dried out, but she found an unopened pot of white makeup and a black grease pencil that still worked.

She took these to the mirror and began to transform her face. After all, Anna thought, it was a Halloween dance. Everyone there would be in disguise.

As Anna smeared the makeup over her skin, she began to have the feeling that she was being watched. Twice she had to turn around to make sure no one was in the room with her, and once she actually went to the window and pressed her nose against the glass to look outside.

"I'm starting to lose it," Anna muttered to herself as she returned to the mirror. "If this keeps up, I really *am* going to go crazy."

She put the final touches on her makeup and stepped back to look at her work. She'd painted her face bone white, with black circles around her eyes. She looked like a cross between a skeleton and a ghoul. It wasn't much of a costume. But it would have to do.

Anna zipped on a sweatshirt and pulled the hood over her head. Then she grabbed a pile of dirty clothes from her laundry hamper and shoved them under her quilt, pushing them into a sort of Anna-shaped lump. Hopefully, if her parents came to check on her, they wouldn't look too closely.

She stuffed some money into her pocket and started for the window. But as she threw it open, she paused.

Was she really doing the right thing, sneaking into the dance like this? There were so many risks. Her parents might discover she was gone. Or Ms. Turk might spot her at the dance.

And what if this was another setup? A chilling new thought occurred to Anna. By showing up at the dance, she might be risking more than suspension — if Emma planned to do something horrible to Dory, surely she also planned to frame Anna for the crime.

I have to take that chance, Anna decided. Emma had already hurt Dory once. She couldn't let her do it again.

Taking a deep breath, Anna climbed onto the windowsill and swung herself out into the night.

When she got to the school, Anna saw a long line outside the door to the gym. She felt a burst of hope. Maybe Dory was still in line. If so, Anna could warn her quickly and be back home before anyone discovered her gone.

Anna began to move forward, alongside the line, looking for her friend among the rubber-masked monsters and mummies wrapped in toilet paper. She saw witches, ghosts, waitresses . . . but no one who looked like they might be Dory.

As Anna passed a girl with ratted black hair, she heard a familiar voice say, "This dance had better be good, because these boots are, like, *killing* my feet."

Anna froze. Cautiously, she peered around the edge of her hood. Jessamyn, Kima, and Lauren were standing next to her in line. They were dressed as a punk band — shredded clothes, black lipstick, studded bracelets, and fake tattoos. Kima even had a length of chain wrapped around her neck.

Anna lowered her head and hurried past, making a wide circle around them.

She worked her way to the front of the line, but she didn't see Dory anywhere. With a sigh, she realized she would have to go inside. The two girls standing at the front of the line were busy talking to each other, so Anna slipped in front of them.

"Five dollars," said the Frankenstein who was taking money at the door.

"Hey!" cried one of the girls behind Anna, who'd suddenly noticed she'd cut in line. "We were next!"

Anna ignored her. She shoved a wad of bills at Frankenstein without bothering to count them.

"You forgot to get your hand stamped!" he called as Anna hurried into the dance.

The strobe-lit gym was a mass of bodies, all jumping up and down to the thumping beat of a hip-hop song. Anna peered at a zombie that staggered past, but in the dim light she couldn't even tell if it was a boy or a girl. How was she ever going to spot Dory — or Emma, for that matter — in here?

She circled the dance floor, inspecting the faces she passed, but she quickly realized it was futile. Between the costumes and dark lighting, she stood little chance of finding anyone in the crowd.

Just then, Anna *did* see someone she recognized. Ms. Turk was standing against the wall of the gym, just a few feet in front of her. The dean's arms were folded across her chest, and she was watching the dancers with a pinched expression.

Anna quickly reversed direction. As she turned back toward the doors, she caught a glimpse of a short figure in a yellow rain jacket. The hood was up, partially covering her face.

"Dory?" Anna murmured.

As she watched, Dory slipped out the side door into the hallway that connected the gym with the main school building. Anna hurried after her.

When she reached the door, she looked out and saw Dory walking purposefully down the darkened hallway. "Dory!" Anna called out. But Dory didn't turn around. She went straight to the old girls' bath-room and disappeared inside.

"What's she doing?" Anna wondered. Had Emma somehow lured her there, away from the crowd, so she could hurt her? With her heart in her throat, Anna pulled open the door.

The bathroom was empty.

She stepped inside, letting the door swing shut behind her. "Dory?" she whispered.

The buzzing of the fluorescent lights was the only reply. One of the bulbs flickered spasmodically, like a dying thing struggling to stay alive.

Anna checked each of the stalls, but they were all empty. The bathroom had no windows and no other door. Anna knew she'd seen Dory come in here. So where was she?

Anna turned to leave, but as she did, she caught a glimpse of her reflection in the bathroom mirror. In the hot gym, her face paint had started to melt, the black and white blending together in greasy gray streaks.

But that wasn't all. Anna pushed her hood back from her face and leaned closer. There was some-thing weird about her eyes. . . .

As she frowned into the mirror, her dark brown eyes suddenly turned silver.

Anna screamed and stumbled backward as Emma separated herself from Anna's reflection.

You see, Anna? You can't run from me. I'm a part of you.

Anna could hear Emma's voice, though not through her ears. This time Emma seemed to be speaking directly to her thoughts.

"Leave me alone!" Anna turned to flee.

But at that second, the door opened. Jessamyn, Kima, and Lauren sauntered in.

"Well, look who's here." Jessamyn put her hands on her hips, her black lips twisting into a wicked smile. "I'm surprised to see you, Anna. Didn't I hear that you were on probation? Maybe I should go get Ms. Turk. I'll bet she'll be *very* interested to know you're here."

Kima and Lauren flanked Jessamyn, like two guard dogs waiting for the command to attack. Kima had unwound the chain from her neck and was swinging it from one hand threateningly.

"On second thought," Jessamyn said, narrowing her eyes, "I knew there was a reason I wore these steel-toed boots tonight." She tapped the toe of her boot against the floor, and Anna heard the hard knock of metal.

She's bluffing, Anna told herself. *They're all bluffing. They wouldn't really try to beat me up, not with the entire school just a few yards away. . . .*

But as the group slowly closed in on her, Anna's confidence vanished. She glanced around for an escape. The only way out was through the door, which the Jackals were blocking.

"I'm going to make you sorry you ever messed with me," Jessamyn snarled.

Anna, another voice broke in, *I'm here for you. Come to me. Come over to my side.*

Anna glanced into the mirror and saw Emma beckoning to her. In that second, her fear of the Jackals overcame her fear of Emma. Anna reached out her hand.

Emma's hand came out of the mirror and grasped her own. The other girls saw it, for they sprang back, and Anna heard their screams. But she wasn't thinking about them anymore.

The moment Emma's hand closed around hers, Anna realized she'd made a mistake. Emma's grip was like steel, and as she pulled Anna toward her, Anna saw the evil in her eyes. In that instant, Anna knew she'd never be able to return to her old life again.

"No!" she cried. But it was too late. Emma was pulling her into the mirror.

Chapter Sixteen

As Anna's hand slid through the mirror and into Emma's world, she felt a coldness that seeped all the way into her bones. The mirror rippled like the surface of a pond into which she would plunge and lose herself forever. Somewhere in the distance, she could hear someone screaming. Or was she herself screaming? In her terror and confusion, Anna couldn't tell.

And then, suddenly, two arms grasped her around the waist and began to pull her backward, away from Emma. For a split second, Anna thought she saw an angel reflected in the mirror. A golden angel with . . . glasses?

Then she recognized the face. It was Dory in her sun costume, her face painted gold, a halo of golden beams sprouting from her headband like rays of sunshine.

"No!" Dory yelled, tugging at Anna with all her might. "You can't have her!"

For a moment, Anna thought her arm would be wrenched out of its socket as Emma fought to hold on to her. But Dory was surprisingly strong for her size. At last she managed to tear Anna from Emma's grip.

In the mirror, Anna saw Emma rear back, her face twisted with greed and fury. As Emma lunged again, Anna snatched the chain out of the stunned Kima's hand. She swung it against the mirror with all her might.

There was an earsplitting crash of breaking glass, then an enraged scream that shook Anna to her core.

And then, nothing.

In the silence that followed, the girls stared at each other.

"Is she gone?" Dory finally managed to squeak.

With the toe of her sneaker, Anna nudged the shards of glass on the tile floor. "I think so."

Behind her she heard a small groan. Anna turned in time to see Jessamyn's eyes roll back in her head . . . right before she crumpled to the floor.

Kima and Lauren glanced between Anna and their fallen comrade. Then they opened the door and ran.

"Nice friends," Dory said with a snort. She looked down at Jessamyn. "What do you say? Should we leave her here?"

"Part of me wants to say yes." Anna sighed. "But that would make me just like her. Besides," she added with a little smile, "I just gave her the scare of her life, didn't I? I want to rub it in a little."

"What I don't understand is, where were you hiding?" Anna asked Dory a short time later.

They were sitting in the hallway outside the gym. Behind them, the dance was still going. Every once in a while the door would open, and they would hear a blast of music.

"I followed you into the bathroom," Anna went on. "I wanted to warn you about Emma. But when I got there, it was like you'd vanished into thin air!"

Dory shook her head. "That doesn't make sense. You couldn't have followed me, because *I* followed *you*. I saw Jessamyn and those girls go into the bathroom behind you. I was afraid they might try something. I didn't know Emma would be there, too."

Anna twisted a loose piece of hair around one finger. "But then how — ?" She broke off as she realized. "It was Emma. She disguised herself as you to fool me. And then she hid in the mirror. She was always in the mirror."

That's why I always felt like I was being watched, Anna thought. *The mirror was her way of spying on me.*

"You really did see something in the mirror that day you fainted in the bathroom, didn't you?" Dory asked.

Anna nodded. She remembered the day of her initiation with the Jackals. She'd called on a spirit in the mirror. But it was Emma who'd answered the call.

"I think that old mirror was some kind of portal," Anna said. "Emma must have realized that she'd never be able to have me all to herself here. So she tried to take me into her world."

"You know earlier today, how you asked me if I remembered Emma?" Dory said. "I did remember her. I just couldn't believe what you were saying."

Anna shrugged. She didn't blame Dory. She'd had trouble believing it herself.

"I was afraid of her when we were little," Dory confessed. "She used to pinch me behind your back. I couldn't even see her then, but I knew she was there."

"She was jealous of you," Anna told her. "She wanted to be my only friend. That's why she pushed you down the stairs. That time you broke your arm."

Dory's eyes widened. "So it did happen! I thought . . ."

"I know," Anna said, nodding. "You thought it couldn't be true."

"After I broke my arm, you stopped talking about Emma," Dory explained. "I remember I mentioned her once, and you told me, 'She's *imaginary*, Dory.' It was like she'd never existed. So after a while, I started to believe I'd imagined the whole thing."

"I must have thought she'd go away if I ignored her," Anna said. "But she didn't really go away. She was there the whole time, just waiting for the chance to come back again."

Dory rubbed her broken collarbone thoughtfully. "I read somewhere about evil spirits that will latch on to a person. You know, kind of like a guardian angel, but bad. Do you think that's what Emma was?"

Anna was silent. She'd been wondering about that. Was Emma an evil spirit — or something Anna had accidentally wished into existence? Anna didn't know. What she did know was that Emma was drawn to her. She fed off Anna's own meanness, insecurity, and doubt. And if that was the case, how could Anna be sure she wouldn't come back?

Because I won't let her, Anna promised herself. *I know her now, and I'll never let her back.*

"I don't want to think about Emma anymore," Anna said firmly. "It's Halloween, and I'm — I'm . . . oh no, I'm *so* busted!" She checked her watch. She'd been gone for over two hours. Her parents would surely have discovered she was missing by now.

She explained to Dory how she'd snuck out the window. "I'm dead meat," she groaned. "What am I going to tell them?"

"I could go with you, if you want," Dory offered. "I'll tell them I had an emergency, and I needed your help. It's sort of true."

Anna shook her head. "It wouldn't matter. I'm still going to be grounded for the rest of my natural-born life. But," she added, "I appreciate the thought."

"Well," Dory said, standing up and dusting off the seat of her costume, "if you're going to be grounded for the rest of your natural-born life, you might as well get in one last dance."

"I really should get home," Anna said.

"Come on, one song," Dory said. "Then you can be grounded for as long as you like. Besides, I want you to meet my new friends. You'll like them." She held out her hand to Anna.

"Okay," Anna agreed, taking it. "One song." She let herself be pulled to her feet. But she didn't let go of her friend's hand right away.

"Thanks, Dory," she said, giving it a squeeze.

"No problem," said Dory. "Besides, I owed you one."

Anna was surprised. "For what?"

"Well, for one thing," Dory said, smiling, "if it weren't for you, I'd be standing here with a scrub brush on my head."

Epilogue

"Three more days to Thanksgiving!" Anna crowed. "I cannot wait!"

It was a Monday, just after fourth period. Anna, Dory, Melody, and Kate had gathered at Anna's locker before they made their way to the cafeteria for lunch.

"I had no idea you liked turkey so much," Melody teased.

"Who cares about turkey?" she replied. "I'm looking forward to the taste of *freedom*."

Her friends laughed. They all knew that Thanksgiving was the day Anna would officially be ungrounded.

"So, what should we do on Anna's first weekend back among the living?" Dory asked the group.

"We could go to a movie," suggested Melody.

"Better yet, we could *make* a movie!" Dory exclaimed. "Hester and Harold are dying to start acting again."

"I say we go to the mall and buy Anna a new mirror for her locker," said Kate, who'd been checking her hair in the one on Anna's locker door. "This one stinks."

"I don't care *what* we do," Anna said, "as long as it's fun."

Just then, she noticed Benny Riveras coming down the hall on crutches. He seemed to be making his way right toward her. Anna suddenly felt nervous. Benny had returned to school a few weeks before, but he'd avoided her. Anna hadn't spoken to him since the day after his accident.

He slowly made his way over to them. "Hi, Anna," he said shyly.

"Hey, Benny." Anna was surprised and pleased. She didn't think Benny was ever going to talk to her again.

Benny glanced uncomfortably at the other girls, and Anna caught his meaning. She turned to her friends. "I'll catch up with you guys in a minute. Save me a seat, okay?"

Dory, Melody, and Kate left, shooting her winking looks, which she ignored. "So, how's your leg?" she asked Benny when they were gone.

"Getting better every day," he told her. "Doctor says I might even be back on skates by January." He shifted on his crutches. "So, listen, I've been meaning to talk to you for a long time. I wanted to apologize."

"*You* want to apologize?" Anna was startled. "What for?"

"For what I said the day you came to visit me, after the accident," Benny told her. "They say sometimes after you hit your head, you can imagine all kinds of crazy things."

Anna bit her lip. "Well, it wasn't *that* crazy —"

"Are you kidding? I must have sounded like a lunatic," Benny insisted. "Anyway, I want to make it up to you. How about a slice at Moxie after school?"

Anna's heart skipped a beat. He was asking her out again — and this time it was on purpose. For a second she wondered if there was some way she could go. Maybe she could make up some excuse? Or sneak out?

Anna shook her head. She was done with sneaking. "I can't," she told Benny regretfully. "I have a ton of homework. And I'm sort of grounded right now."

"Really? What for?" Benny asked.

Anna sighed. "It's kind of a long story. But," she added quickly, "I'd love to go to Moxie another time."

"Really?" Benny let out a sigh of relief. "I was afraid you'd hate me, after what I said."

Anna shook her head. "Not a chance."

The hall had mostly cleared out. Everyone was already in the cafeteria. "Walk with me to lunch?" Benny asked.

"Yeah, hold on. Let me just get my lunch money." Anna reached into her backpack and pulled out a few bills from a zippered pocket. As she turned to close her locker, she caught a sight of her reflection in the mirror on the door.

For a split second, her reflection seemed to waver, and Anna thought she glimpsed two silver eyes watching her.

That's right, Emma, she thought. *Eat your heart out.* Then she slammed the door shut.

BITE INTO THE NEXT POISON APPLE,
IF YOU DARE. . .

HERE'S A
SPINE-TINGLING SNEAK PEEK!

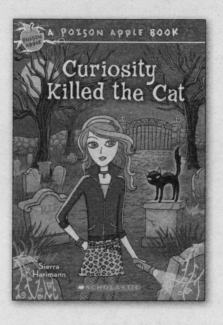

Hannah was alone in her new room, unpacking her things. She had just finished arranging her shoes in the closet when she felt a sudden chill. Goosebumps swept up her arms, and the hairs on the back of her neck prickled. She was sure someone was watching her. Hannah whipped around. Sure enough, Madison stood in the doorway, arms crossed and a nasty scowl on her face.

"Dinner's ready," she snapped at Hannah. Then she sauntered casually into the room. She picked up a black cat figurine Hannah had placed on the dresser. Madison turned it over in her hand and gave it a tiny toss into the air. Hannah gasped as Madison caught the figurine easily with a mean little laugh. She placed it back on the dresser, not very gently.

"I heard about your cat," Madison said, her eyes narrowing. "That's too bad." It didn't sound like she thought it was too terrible, though. In fact, Hannah thought Madison sounded almost gleeful.

Madison took a step closer.

"Let's get a few things straight around here," she said menacingly. "See that door over there?" She gestured over her shoulder.

Hannah nodded.

"That's the door to *my* bathroom," Madison explained. "My mom said I have to let you use it, too." She rolled her eyes dramatically. "But since the only way in is through this room or my bedroom, you'd better remember to unlock my door when you're done in there," Madison continued. "Because if you lock me out of my own bathroom, I will *not* be happy."

"Okay, fine," Hannah squeaked softly. "Can we go eat dinner now?"

"One more thing," Madison said. "If you ever touch even a drop of my shampoo, conditioner, body lotion, or anything else in there, you will be sorry. See you later, *sis*."

And with that, Madison turned and strode out of the room. *Talk about an evil stepsister!* Hannah thought. It was as if Madison had been taking lessons from Cinderella's tormentors.

After a painfully awkward dinner of meat loaf and green-bean casserole (not exactly Hannah's favorites), Hannah was eager to go to bed. She didn't think the day could get any worse, and the sooner she fell asleep, the sooner the day would be over.

Even though it was only 8:30, Hannah pulled on her pajamas, grabbed her toothbrush, and headed for the bathroom. She jiggled the doorknob but it didn't budge, so she tried knocking. There was no answer. Hannah flopped down on her bed to wait. As soon as she did, her phone chimed. It was a text from Paisley.

wanna skype?

OMG! yes! logging on now.

Hannah quickly booted up her computer and logged in to the video chat program. She accepted the incoming call from Paisley, and her best friend's face filled the computer screen.

"Hey!" Paisley waved at her friend. "How's the new place?"

Hannah moved her head so Paisley could see the room behind her. "See for yourself."

"Um, nice posters," Paisley joked. "I didn't realize you were so into basketball. Are you going out for the team?"

"Ha, ha." Hannah stuck out her tongue at Paisley. "Today hasn't been the best day of my life, that's for sure."

"Oh, no! What happened?" Paisley asked, her brow furrowed with concern.

"Well, first Icky ran out of the house while my mom and I were trying to get him into his crate."

Paisley gasped. "That is totally tragic! But you got him back, right?"

"I don't know," Hannah replied glumly. "Hopefully he's back at my mom's by now, but he was still missing when I left. He runs off every now and then, but he never stays out overnight. My mom's going to bring him here tomorrow on her way to the airport."

"I'm so sorry, Hannah." Paisley spread her arms out wide. "Virtual hug!"

"Thanks," Hannah replied softly. "Things didn't get much better after that. Madison's been, well, Madison. And you probably can't see out the window behind me, but you'll never guess what you can see from my bedroom."

Paisley shook her head. "You're right — I have no idea."

Hannah lowered her voice. "It's the Sleepy Hollow Cemetery!"

"Oh, that is *creepy*!" Paisley replied with a shudder. "You've heard the stories they tell about that place, right?"

Hannah nodded. "Yeah, but they're all pretty silly. And it's not like I actually know anyone who's ever been haunted, and I've lived around here for twelve years."

"Well . . ." Paisley began hesitantly and then paused. "There is *one* story about a ghost cat. I don't want to freak you out, though."

Hannah had heard of the ghost cat before, but

she couldn't remember the details. She could tell Paisley knew the story and wanted to tell her, though. Paisley tended to believe in all of the Sleepy Hollow legends way more than Hannah did.

"No, it's okay," Hannah replied gamely. "You'd better tell me. I'd rather be prepared than surprised when a ghost shows up on the front porch."

"Okay, you asked for it," Paisley warned, but Hannah could tell her friend was thrilled to be playing the role of storyteller. "So, the legend is that there was a little girl who lived in Sleepy Hollow in, like, the eighteen hundreds. She had this little black cat that followed her around everywhere. Then one day, she and the cat both disappeared. It was, like, poof, they were gone!

"They were missing for days, until some townspeople found the girl's dead body in the Hudson. No one ever saw the cat again, though — well, at least not alive."

Paisley shuddered and lowered her voice dramatically. Even though Hannah knew it was just a story, she felt chills shoot up her spine. The wind outside rustled the leaves of the trees in the yard, and a cool breeze wafted through the window.

Hannah glanced over her shoulder at the window involuntarily, but there was nothing there.

"You sure are good at telling ghost stories, Pais," Hannah said with a nervous laugh.

"And I'm not even done yet!" Paisley continued, her voice a hushed whisper. "The little girl was buried in the Sleepy Hollow cemetery. Supposedly, the ghost of the cat still haunts her grave. Some of the townspeople think the cat had something to do with the girl's drowning. And this is the craziest part — you know my aunt Suzie and my cousin Clark, who live in Stamford?"

Hannah nodded.

"Well, before I was born, they lived in Sleepy Hollow, probably pretty close to your dad's house. I know it was near the cemetery. Anyway, one day the basement of their house totally flooded — *and there hadn't even been a rainstorm!*"

Paisley paused dramatically again, and Hannah laughed.

"Maybe one of the pipes had burst," Hannah pointed out. "That happened in my mom's house a few years ago, and it definitely wasn't because of a ghost."

"Well, that's what they thought at first," Paisley said ominously. "But you'll never guess what they found floating in the water in the basement."

Hannah felt her heartbeat quicken. "What?" she squeaked.

Paisley's voice was deadly serious.

"A drowned black cat."

Petal Pushers

Four sisters.
One flower shop.
Will disaster bloom?

Too Many Blooms   Flower Feud   Best Buds

Don't miss any of these fresh, sweet reads!

read them all!

Life, Starring Me!

Callie for President

Drama Queen

I've Got a Secret

Confessions of a Bitter Secret Santa

Super Sweet 13

The Boy Next Door

The Sister Switch

Snowfall Surprise

Rumor Has It

The Sweetheart Deal

The Accidental Cheerleader

The Babysitting Wars

Star-Crossed

Accidentally
Fabulous

Accidentally
Famous

Accidentally
Fooled

Accidentally
Friends

How to Be a Girly Girl in
Just Ten Days

Ice Dreams

Juicy Gossip

Making Waves

Miss Popularity

Miss Popularity
Goes Camping

Miss Popularity
and the Best Friend Disaster

Totally Crushed

Wish You Were Here,
Liza

See You Soon,
Samantha

Miss You, Mina

Winner Takes All

POISON APPLE BOOKS

The Dead End

This Totally Bites!

Miss Fortune

Now You See Me...

Midnight Howl

Her Evil Twin

THRILLING. BONE-CHILLING. THESE BOOKS HAVE BITE!